UNDERCOVER ALLIANCE

The Confederacy Treaty Book 3

LILLY CAIN

Lilly Cain

Undercover Alliance

Spies. Even in space there is a need for us, men and women undercover to protect our country - and now our planet. I am Starforce Special Agent John Norton. There is someone out to ruin the chances of the treaty between Earth and the Confederacy, but I'm not going to let that happen. Even if they have me under the watchful eye of a powerful Inarrii warrioress. I will do what I must. And if I need to distract her…it won't be too hard on me. In fact it might be too easy…

Saddled with babysitting a man who is no better than a librarian. What a way for a previous war commander to end her career. I am *Soryen* Sarina Tariim - injured in battle but not a complete invalid. There is something not quite right about this assignment. About this man, with his intense eyes and agility no librarian should have. I will learn his secrets and protect the treaty.

The treaty is nearly ready to be signed. But there are forces intent on keeping the Humans and Inarrii apart. It's time for an Undercover Alliance.

Part Three of the Confederacy Treaty

Undercover Alliance
The Confederation Treaty Series Book 3

Lilly Cain

ISBN 978-1-989138-05-2

Cover design by Candace Phillips Gilmer
Flirtation Designs

Discover other titles by Lilly Cain www.lillycain.com

To my readers: Welcome back to the Confederacy Treaty series, where the fates of Earth and the Confederacy lie in the hands of lovers from different worlds. Despite their differences, or perhaps because of them, the strength gained from passion and love must be enough to change everything.

To see more of my work or to contact me, please visit www.lillycain.com.

Chapter 1

"You've got company," Davis's tense voice called through the comm unit.

"No shit." Starforce Special Agent John Norton glanced down at the hull of the ship. The metal still glowed red where it had been struck by laser fire only a few feet away from his position.

John tracked the small fighter skimming close to the long hull of the Starship *Osprey*. Its dark metal body nearly matched the blackness of space. It was coming back for another shot. Twisting, John fired his hand laser. It sheared through the vacuum of space and pierced the edge of the attacker's hull. Dodging return fire, he leaped for the communication array pod at the far end of the ship and hoped like hell his aim was good and his magnetic boots would clamp, or he'd be hurtling into space like garbage. Since no one was going to admit he was even on board, there was no chance of rescue. His heart pounded, his breath rasping loudly inside the confines of his polarized helmet. He turned and fired again. This time the laser hit a crucial spot, and the small craft peeled off from its attack course.

John released the laser, allowing it to dangle from his wrist strap, and gripped the ship as his boots hit and clamped tight to the edge of the array. Leaning into the small amount of shelter provided by the communication pod, he scanned above him. Only one sleek, little fighter had gone for him, its design confirming what he'd already been told. There was more to the terrorist group Terran Purity than a ragtag group of human racists. The fighter was too sophisticated to be of Earth origin. The *Osprey* hadn't picked it up, or Davis would have caught that on the online chatter. That meant the attacker had some serious shielding. The terrorist shouldn't have detected John either —a single moving figure on the exterior of the massive human Starship *Osprey*, his suit designed to deflect not only the coldness of space but any heat or ultrasonic detection. At least, that was the plan.

Quickly he flipped open the closest access panel and toggled the manual relay on the communications pod. Two more minutes and he would have the fourth and final bug in place. Not that he could rely on the listening devices any longer. No one in Starforce should have known he was here, let alone the Purity assholes. Someone could be aware of the surveillance equipment he was planting as well. Any information he got from them would be suspect at best. He pulled the bug from his forearm pocket and pressed it against the console. He felt it dissolve into the circuitry through the pressure-sensitive fingerpads on his suit and suppressed a shudder. It never failed to revolt him the way the damn bugs could work their way through anything electronic, and he vowed again to refuse the microcircuit brain implants the brass had been pushing on all upper-level agents.

Motion flickered in the corner of his eye. Instantly he snapped off the magnetic clamps in his boots and shoved away from the array. Laser fire bit into the hull inches away from where he'd been locked on. He fired the narrow jets on his back, the silent explosion of compressed gas propelling him away from the array and back toward his only exit without a hint of heat to give away his location.

The fucking fighter was back, its maneuverability amazing as it followed him across the underbelly of the ship.

John grabbed at his dangling laser and flicked a shot across what he guessed was the view panel of the pilot. He snapped the magnets back on his boots, slamming into the hull. The fighter's momentum pulled the ship past his location, and he shot the laser at full capacity, directly at what had to be a rear power nodule.

In a flash of light, the back of the fighter ship ripped forward through its front.

John gasped. An explosion was not what he'd expected. The resulting shockwave flashed toward him, driving him back against the hull in a way that made him twist and shout out in sudden pain. Then the blackness of space claimed the final charred remains of the attacker.

Panting for breath, John weighed his options. His knee radiated agony. There wouldn't be much time before someone came to investigate the explosion. The *Osprey* captain would already be aware of the attack, although hopefully not what had caused the terrorist ship to detonate. They'd be looking for answers. John straightened and forced himself to bring up his helmet comp unit and signal for a map. It flared to life across his visor, the light color of the map illuminating his screen with a sudden flare of pain behind his eyes. The explosion had left his head throbbing and his knee feeling as though he'd been kicked, hard.

"Fuck."

"I heard that, Norton. Good to know you're alive. Now get your ass in here."

"I'm working on it, Davis. Keep your pants on." John's map pointed the way and a quick pulse from his jet pushed him toward the closest service hatch.

"Trust me, I wouldn't go anywhere near you without my pants." The deep voice of his mission tech radiated good humor. The man had a sick sense of what was funny in the middle of the most dangerous of missions. If it wasn't for John's strict rule—no partners—he might have taken the man out for a few drinks and laughs. But keeping things professional and separate had saved his ass more than once. Connections only made things more complicated.

"I keep telling you, Davis—you're not my type."

"Far as I can see, you haven't got a type. And you have three minutes before the security team reaches that hatch. Move your ass."

John didn't reply. His knee throbbed now with every heartbeat. In space he didn't have to put his weight on it. Inside the ship it was going to be a bitch to put any speed on and avoid arrest by the very people he was actually protecting. He had to get back to his cover assignment. He reached the hatch and yanked it open. Davis would have already triggered the lock release from wherever the hell he was, via remote link. Now would come the hard part.

SORYEN SARINA TARIIM slammed a fist into the oral port of her charging attacker. The lean alien went down in a graceless collapse, only to be replaced by another, and another. They swarmed her, their stinking, slimy skin repulsive as they tried to push her to the soggy ground and rip her limb from limb. She grabbed one creature's arm and slammed him into the next, kicking a third in its midsection. Still more of them darted toward her. All they had to do was pull her breather from her face and she'd be dead in minutes. Around her other Inarrii fought hand to hand against the Archat swarm. Lasers were useless and actually dangerous to fire in the methane-rich atmosphere of this world.

She'd lost her first set of *dash'tet* knives and now reached for her second, grabbing for the hilts strapped to her calves. The movement cost her; two more Archat were on her in seconds but she rolled with their attack, using their momentum to skewer them through on her long *dash'tet*.

A long hooting howl sounded as she pulled her knives from their bodies. The unprovoked attack on the Inarrii scout party was now a retreat. Inarrii all around her raised their voices in a ragged cheer, and she laughed aloud.

Too soon, the feeling of exhilaration melted away. Her grin faded. This was useless. There was no real victory. She didn't know the Inarrii warrior who had battled only a few feet away. He wasn't her teammate and this wasn't real. With a decisive slash of her *dash'tet*, still dripping with alien gore, she shut down the battle simulator and stepped out of the holo unit. Her battle gear faded as she exited, but the bruising she'd received inside the simulation remained painfully real.

Fighting these images, these pale reflections of old battles, provided only a few moments of relief from the truth. She'd been there, on the very mission this simulation had been based on. She'd fought on dozens of worlds, performed hundreds of dangerous missions. But it would never be the same. She rubbed the upper muscle of her left arm, felt the damage no Inarrii medtech would ever be able to remove.

Beneath the fading scar tissue was the real injury. Her *L'inar* were severed, the damage far deeper than surface lacerations. Despite a dozen reconstructive surgeries, her synapses no longer meshed. She would never again have complete release, experience the utter sexual abandon the sensitive *L'inar* nerve lines could inspire. And without that completion, her mind was at risk. At least, according to Inarrii belief.

Her therapist said she would recover. Her commander agreed. Her clan was sympathetic, but already garnering the political credit and honor points from a permanent disability of one of their own in the line of duty. Her current assignment indicated her clan was more in touch with reality than either of her advisors.

Sarina exited the simulation lounge of the Inarrii flagship Horneu. This would be her last evening on board before she headed to her new assignment and complete boredom. There would be no more laser fights in her future, no space battles. With a groan, she walked to the next section of the training level. The familiar and usually comforting scent of sweat in the strength focus room did nothing to cool the anger that burned inside her over her predicament. She could fly a ship, strategize and fight with the best, excel at everything a warrior could hope for, but she would never get the chance to prove it again. Just because her damn *L'inar* and her lack of a sex life were a supposed threat to her sanity.

"Fuck." She tested the human curse and found it vaguely satisfying, and in her situation the curse was ironically apt. She moved over to the resistance boards and attached the wrist and ankle straps. Throwing her weight and her anger into the workout, she pushed herself to the limit.

The boards hummed with power as she strained to touch them, to press them past her usual level. Sweat beaded on her back, slowly slipping down the length of her spine. Her *L'inar* reacted to the slight touch of the drops of liquid. Sensation fizzled along the nerves, flared around the curve of her ribs, bounced erratically around her abdomen to flicker over the lower curve of her breasts, only to dissipate. She jerked in her restraints, the sensation an erotic tease, a reminder of the fact that she hadn't had sex in a month and wasn't likely to experience it any time soon.

She ripped the bands from her wrists and glanced around the room, thankful the area remained nearly empty. Perhaps they were right. Even if she managed to reach orgasm again, these unpredictably odd flashes of *L'inar* activity just might drive her insane. At least no one had witnessed her strange reaction. One set of warriors trained in hand-to-hand combat in the far corner of the training level. Their strikes and parries nearly blurred in rapid progression. They were in sync with each other, even their breaths matching rhythms. Sarina pulled off her ankle straps, never taking her eyes off the sparring couple. They had to be a couple. If they weren't, they soon would be. The flashing blows were slowing, becoming more of a dance than an attack. Before the night was out, they would be wrapped in a dance of a different kind. Skin on sweaty skin.

Sarina sagged against the resistance boards. Their power had disengaged the moment she pulled off the tethers. Inert now, they bowed slightly with her weight. Perhaps leaving the Horneu wouldn't be such a bad thing. Despite the incredible boredom of guarding a human nobody, at least on the human ships there was no open sex. No erotic displays, no direct offers that held the intimacy of *m'ittar* mind contact and a promise that couldn't be fulfilled—complete *L'inar* arousal and release.

She turned away from the couple and walked quietly from the room to the sonic cleansers. The hum of the cleansing units passed their vibration up through the soles of her feet and into her body. An ache low in her belly reminded her again, as if she needed any more reminders, that it had been weeks since she'd shared the tension-relieving experience of sex. Without sex, Inarrii could not de-stress.

That was the reason she was being assigned to body-guard such a low-status human. What would they have done with her if she hadn't already learned standard English? No de-stressing meant an eventual breakdown, but how much stress could she experience guarding John Bennings, a lawyer who spent his days deep in the tangled webs of information completing the final layer of the human/Confederation Treaty?

It was a horrifyingly dull thought.

Still, a job was a job. And as long as she could, she'd retain the rank of warrior, a *Soryen*, giving every assignment everything she had. Anyone who said she couldn't could…

fuck themselves. She snickered at her own sick sense of humor and then leaned into the sonic cleanser.

"SPECIAL AGENT NORTON, your mission is simple. Continue with your cover as John Bennings, midlevel lawyer and contract specialist. We'll feed you all the documentation you'll need to work your way through the negotiations, but as the inside man you will be the final line against these terrorists. This Treaty must go through. Earth needs this agreement. It hasn't become common knowledge yet, but with your clearance you must be aware of the alien forces we've been tracking throughout the system." Commander-In-Chief Johaness motioned toward the information displayed across the room.

John rotated in his seat to observe the vid panel on the conference room wall. The seamless flow of information across its microthin surface wasn't new. He was aware the Inarrii weren't the only nonhumans in the area, but it was surprising that information on the number of craft now visible on the outer edges of the galaxy wasn't spread across every news vid on the planet. There were a lot of them, far too many. These had to be the Raveners that the Inarrii had warned would follow in their wake, looking for any undefended planet whose resources were up for the taking. They were moving in, faster than anyone had expected, at least according to the scrolling data.

John turned back to the CIC. She was a tall, thin-boned woman, almost raw in her severity, but the commander-in-chief held more power than most people could dream of. Their eyes met.

He made a slight nod. "The terrorist group Terran Purity—they are still confirmed as the driving force behind the recent attacks on the Inarrii and the negotiating boards?"

"Yes, but intel from several sources has indicated that

the Raveners, in particular the Gathan, a high-tech race rejected by the Confederacy and probably bearing a grudge, have been secretly supplying Terran Purity with advanced firepower." She nodded at the screen, where a picture of a blue-skinned being flickered across the surface, followed by several weapons schematics. "Your recent spacewalk confirmed it."

John studied a nasty-looking laser cannon. "That could rip a hole right through a shuttle."

"Exactly." The CIC slid a small metallic item toward him. "This is a little something new of our own. A portable force shield. I hope you don't need to give it a trial run any time soon."

John picked the tiny generator up, noted the thumbprint and DNA control on the end. They would have already keyed it to his pattern. That they would give him a prototype defense item underlined the gravity and the danger inherent in his mission. "You expect further attacks."

"Yes. Intel has indicated not only increasing frontal assaults of the type we've seen over the last month but also more insidious strikes against the negotiation personnel of both the Inarrii and the human contingents." She snapped off the vid and turned away, taking her seat behind the huge mahogany desk against the back wall of the conference room. "There are only two steps left before the Treaty is complete. The Human Accord—the agreement of every major human political party to go ahead with the Treaty—and the Treaty signing itself." She rubbed the back of her neck, a rare expression of worry and a real measure of the increasing danger.

"While we've taken every precaution, upgraded every level of security, we know there'll be more attacks, and that some may succeed. But no one will be aware of your presence. No one but myself and your immediate commander. You'll be there, standing shoulder to shoulder with the men and women who are building our future in the galaxy. You'll ensure that they've got their chance."

John stood. "Understood." He turned to leave but she caught his attention with a small sound, the simple clearing of her throat.

"Special Agent Norton. One last thing. The Inarrii know nothing of your position. But your cover, along with every other human legal representative, has been assigned an Inarrii bodyguard. They, like us, are taking no chances."

John nodded. The complication was minor. "I'm sure they've done what they see as aid for us without completely taxing their resources. A bodyguard is not a problem."

"Let's hope not, Agent. There can be no distractions, and no interference with your mission."

FIRST IMPRESSIONS COULD SAY a lot about a person, but observation of a subject when he was at ease, following a routine he was familiar with, told far more. Sarina studied her charge carefully as he worked. The meeting had been in session for an hour since the last intermission. She'd been introduced briefly to John Bennings by the captain of the *Osprey* during their meal break. Benning's handshake had been firm, and his height and muscular frame belied a life of facts and figures. With his powerful, lean muscles, his body spoke more of the strength brought on by hard exercise, perhaps even some human form of hand-to-hand combat. It also spoke softly, seductively of sex.

His hands were long-fingered. He wore a well-tailored white shirt and dark pants, but he'd turned back the cuffs on his sleeves almost to his elbows. Fine, light brown hairs along his exposed forearms caught her attention and held it as she considered where else he might have such silken decoration. He wore the hair on his head short, not like the long locks of a male Inarrii warrior. But there was something about the way he carried himself. He reminded her of someone.

"And that's enough for today. Thank you everyone. We'll meet again tomorrow." The human chairman stood up from the meeting table. "I'll remind you that we have two weeks until the next meeting of the Treaty negotiation boards. We've been making good progress, but there is still a long way to go to finalize the agreements on Earth before the signing of the first Intergalactic Treaty." He smiled, but clearly the rest of the team had been dismissed.

The lawyers and legal aids began shuffling about, most packing up their datapads and styluses or tapping shut their coms. Not Bennings. He sat still as the rest moved on as a pack, the humans and their unobtrusive Inarrii guards. She watched him watching them until her gaze caught his attention.

He studied her and she returned the look. His eyes were a soft gray, not blue or brown like the few humans she'd met so far, and no where near her own verdant green, the most common Inarrii color. His eyes were beautiful. And it didn't matter.

She broke the connection and looked around the room, scanning the exits and the few people still within the area.

"Sergeant Tariim." He used the human equivalent of her Inarrii rank of *Soryen* and he spoke softly, but she caught the deep timbre of his voice beyond its hushed tones. "I'm beat. I'm going back to my quarters. I won't be going anywhere, so you can stand down. Get settled in. I'm sure they've quartered you somewhere near my rooms."

He'd gotten close to her without making a sound. She'd been aware of his movements, but if she hadn't been paying attention, would she have even noticed that he'd stepped closer, let alone come within striking distance of her? *Interesting.* Even the spongy shoes most humans wore on board ship usually made some noise. Their height was close; she looked directly into his eyes without shifting her stance. A quick flicker of awareness passed over her. For an instant she wondered if he could have some form of *m'ittar*; it was common knowledge that some humans had proven their ability to share thoughts and emotions, at least to some degree. This is what made them such attractive possible members for the Confederacy.

"Actually, I have had our rooms reassigned. Our quarters are now on the third deck, sector two." She stated the fact and ignored the flash of attraction that raced through her as she inhaled his muted scent. He smelled of fresh rain along the beach line of her home world. Like an ocean breeze.

"Reassigned." His eyes took on a steely note. "You've had our rooms reassigned together? As in, sharing the rooms?"

"We have adjoining quarters. I cannot guard you from the opposite end of the ship. I will not be…settling in. My shift doesn't end until the Treaty is compete and I am transferred."

For a moment she thought he might argue with her. A tiny line of tension formed along the corner of his full mouth. She took a quick breath as the old excitement flickered through her muscles. A fight would be good. A little excitement on a surely boring tour of duty. Perhaps if it became physical they would send her back to the Horneu. *And what would you do there?* a silent voice whispered within her.

But he broke off eye contact, lowered his gaze to flicker briefly over her body before he nodded. "Fine. I'm sure you know what you're doing."

He'd deferred to her. A strange feeling of disappointment settled into her stomach. She shook her head and led the way out of the conference room and through the corridor to the ship's central lift. What did she think a data-shuffling tech would do, challenge her for dominance? Maybe she was already beginning to lose her mind. She needed his compliance if she expected to protect him. In a dangerous situation, she had to know he would follow her lead. She considered the slight hesitation, the line of tension beside his mouth before he'd accepted the room change. Perhaps he would follow her. Perhaps not. As long as it didn't get to that point it didn't matter, and after the mind-numbingly boring meeting she'd just observed, surely no one would be interested in attacking this level of tedious bureaucracy.

Chapter 2

A nother speech. Sarina held back the groan that threatened to rumble free of her throat. The second call for assembly chimed on the comm, and she caught John Bennings staring at her, waiting for her to make a move toward the hallway that would take them to the common galley. She considered skipping the assembly, telling her charge that it was too risky to attend every meeting, but as she thought about it, he seemed to hone in on her hesitation. He raised an eyebrow at her, a smile hinting at the corner of his mouth.

He knew she was bored. It had to be easy to see, despite the fact that she tried to keep it discreet. All she had to hear was another rousing speech on why the humans were making the monumental effort to agree on the Treaty and form the first-ever Human Accord and she would lose her patience completely. Apparently, humans never agreed on anything when there were more than a dozen of them in a room. Two days of observing the legal ramblings that preceded the Accord were enough proof of that. Of course, a warring race could mean more warriors to join the Inarrii clans.

Sarina took a deep breath before she made the first step toward the common galley. Anything that inspired the humans to complete their work and be ready, finally, to sign a Treaty with the Confederacy would be worth it.

"At least it won't be another minor religious dignitary weighing in on how they've been predicting this moment for decades." John's whisper would barely be audible to a human; she was the only Inarrii in the area. His words told her he was already aware of her decision to take him to the meeting. His inflection told her he understood how little she wanted to attend. She didn't respond, but he continued anyway. "I heard the new Inarrii ambassador team is speaking today."

Sarina sucked in a breath. The ambassador team would include former examiner Asler Kiis and his new mate, a human pilot—the same one who'd been part of the cause of her injury. Her anger had abated about the human captain, especially since her trial had revealed how badly she'd been tortured and how bravely she had acted, but the idea of seeing her in person again, now healed and on the arm of a powerful Inarrii lover, was not a happy one.

"What's wrong?" John's whisper was louder, closer. He'd moved to walk closer to her, and she realized that she was projecting her anxiety. Even if he couldn't sense her *m'ittar,* he could probably recognize the displeasure in her expression.

She relaxed and glanced over at him. He seemed concerned, but he quickly cleared his face as the hallway began to fill with people.

"It's nothing."

"Asler Kiis...he was once an Examiner...a lawyer of sorts?"

She gave a short, barking laugh. "You could say that, but I do not think it applies in the way you think. Examiners are lawyers, judges, executioners. They are therapists and warriors. Healers, occasionally."

"Healers?"

They were almost at the entrance of the common area.

She scanned the room and the gathering of people. This would be a perfect moment for an attack, with many of the negotiators gathered here, and the most recognizable human/Inarrii couple to date as speakers. People feared the result of the mating. Although no child could be born of the couple, ideas were spreading.

She motioned to the corner of the room, close to an escape route, should one be necessary. Bennings followed her direction, something she didn't think about until they were seated. She'd used wordless military hand signals; Bennings had recognized and followed her instructions without a single second guess.

As the noise from the small crowd increased, she leaned in closer to her charge. "The Examiners sometimes work to heal minds."

"And now he's partnered with a woman who was tortured, but he isn't an Examiner anymore. Must be difficult."

Sarina studied John's face. A tiny line of tension spoke of something in his past that might not like being tied to a partner who couldn't hold his or her own. "Captain Branscombe has been healed. They would not be mated otherwise. And although Kiis cannot hold the position of Examiner, since he was forced to expose memories during her trial, the talent is part of him. No doubt they make for an excellent team."

"Perhaps." His lips pressed tightly together. Sarina recognized the look. He had memories, and sorrows, of his own.

THIS WAS A COLOSSAL MISTAKE. Day three into the most uneventful mission he'd ever experienced, and he'd succumbed to the urge to do *something*. Anything. But this had probably been the worst choice he could have made.

John stared across the room at Sarina's taut body. She

was experimenting with the human weight machines. It was clear she could handle herself; that showed in the way she walked and held herself, with an ease born of years of combat training. He'd read her dossier, knew the number of battles she'd participated in. But upon seeing her bench-press more than he could have done back in the days when he'd actually cared for muscle mass over speed, the point was driven home.

If he took this to the next level, tried her out in the ring with some simple sparring, she might even kick his ass. But that was something he couldn't risk anyway. Bad enough coming into the gym, but sparring in public would definitely do damage to his cover. What kind of lawyer fought hand to hand with his bodyguard? None. But he'd seen the way she looked longingly at the padded mats. A couple of guys grappled on the blue pads, tossing each other and working to perfect their karate falls. She missed the action as much as he did. Or maybe she just wanted the men.

John pushed harder against the weight machine, thrusting his strength and frustration into his workout. While he would never actively wish for action, he'd had a lot of time to think. And since he'd gone over his mission a hundred times in the last two days, he didn't have much to think about except Sarina. She was staring at the sparring ring, absently rubbing her hand over the upper biceps of her other arm. The man in him admired her body; the agent wondered what she was thinking and whether she knew how often she touched the scars on her arm and shoulder.

He let go of the weights, forgetting for a moment that in the accelerated gravity of the gym they would drop with a heavy clank. He sensed Sarina's eyes on him, could practically feel her getting closer.

"Are you growing tired?" Her voice sounded calm, uncensored, but he wondered if she was amused at the "lawyer" giving up so soon.

"No, but I am getting a little bored. I prefer to run for exercise, but there isn't space on board the ship."

"You could use the running machine."

He glanced over at the treadmill. "It's not the same."

"I understand. Nothing moves. Everything stays the same around you. There is no challenge."

"Exactly." John studied her. She surprised him again with another astute observation. That was exactly why he hated the treadmill. He'd just never thought about it before. Of course, he'd never had time to think about it before.

"We could hit the sheets."

"What?" That thought had his full attention.

"The sheets? The fighting sheets over there?"

"Ah. I think your English finally ran out. Those are mats. Fighting ring. Not sheets. Sheets are bed coverings."

She didn't blush over her mistake, although he could see immediately that she understood what she'd implied. The Inarrii were hardly embarrassed by sexual innuendos. But the lines on her neck and exposed arms rippled, reminding him they were not the brownish tattoos they resembled. They were *L'inar*, sensory nerve lines that covered most of her body. They could be indicating sexual desire. Or anger, or any strong emotion.

John turned away from their hypnotic movement and gathered his brains back from the southward direction they'd fled to, thinking of hitting the sheets—hell, hitting anything with Sarina. Any place, any time. He'd already imagined wrestling with her on the mats, building up heat and sweat until their skin became slippery…

"Are you well, Mr. Bennings?"

"Ah, I think I'm tired after all. Perhaps we should return to the rooms. I have some work to do." John began to wipe himself down with a small towel. A shower, a cold shower, was definitely in order.

Sarina followed him as he moved toward the gym exit.

She hadn't even broken a sweat. "Exercise is important, Mr. Bennings."

"John, please."

"John. Perhaps you need a sparring partner."

The words were a bit too close to his thoughts. "I prefer to work alone." He walked on, having memorized the maze of ship corridors before he'd come on board.

She followed, not commenting. He realized for the first time in days she was letting him lead, and wondered if she'd realized he knew his way around the ship as well as she did. He considered how many ways he might have given her hints over the last couple of days that he was not who he pretended to be. The thought cooled him faster than a cold shower.

He made a motion to open the door to their suite.

She stopped him before he could toggle the entry. "Me first, Mr. Bennings. You know the rules."

He let her take the lead. Face any danger that might be there. It was her job, after all. But it was weird. He hadn't trusted anyone in years and every time she put herself in front of him, he felt...displaced. It was his cover, but he preferred to trust only himself.

JOHN ROLLED TO HIS SIDE. The sheets on the bed wouldn't stay put. He groaned and rolled to the other side, tangling them further. The blanket was long gone. He'd tried to beat his pillow into submission some time ago, but it hadn't helped. It was somewhere near oh-two-hundred in the morning and he was wide-awake. Giving up on the pretense of sleep, he signaled the bedside comp to engage a dim overhead light.

He'd been aboard the *SS Osprey* for three days. Three long, boring days after the initial excitement of the sneak attack on his quick spacewalk and meeting with the CIC. Each day Davis fed him information, and he worked through the data with the rest of the legal team. So far there hadn't been a hitch, no question of his background and no sign of any terrorist threat. Slowly the team was working through the excruciating detail of the Human Accord, which had to be signed before the human/Inarrii Treaty could be completed. If it hadn't been for his bodyguard, he might have died from boredom.

He flung an arm up and behind his head. Already his cock stood in stiff attention at the mere thought of Sarina and her tight body. She was gorgeous. He was also certain she thought he was the closest thing to a cold fish she'd ever experienced. At least, that was his guess. He made a point to agree to every security precaution she suggested, keeping to his quiet, studious cover. Excitement, especially the kind that could come with arguing with such a powerful, beautiful woman like Sarina, wasn't on his list of mission outcomes. And her demands were exactly what he would insist upon if he were in her shoes, guarding a foreign dignitary.

But God, he'd like to make a few demands of his own. She wouldn't imagine him as a cold fish then. He'd like to show her how exciting he could be. Hit the sheets. Like to give her a taste of excitement, take her on a spacewalk, maybe even reveal his true identity…

Whoa, boy. Even in a fantasy that isn't such a good idea. Obviously the monotony was getting to him. He turned his thoughts to the way the curve of her ass was impossible to ignore in her fitted shipsuit.

Unable to resist, he stroked his cock. He was used to action, perhaps even addicted to it, and all this data wrangling for the Treaty left only one outlet for his impulses. Sex.

According to intel, Inarrii didn't just like sex, they needed it as some sort of psychological outlet. She was probably aware of his desire. They were also reported to have varying levels of telepathy and empathy. The brass believed that Starforce Agency training in mental discipline would probably protect him from anything but direct telepathy, but since he'd spent the last three nights fantasizing about screwing her every way possible, she must have picked up on it. Must know he wanted her and was more than willing to take care of any need she might have. But she hadn't reacted, hadn't indicated she needed anything at all from him other than compliance to her security precautions. His cover worked too well.

Not that he had noticed her interest lingering on anyone else on board, at least not before their foray into the gym. From everything he understood about the Inarrii sexual drive, that seemed a bit odd. Perhaps she had special training, or was repulsed by humans in general. But she didn't show any signs of that either. Just a stoicism that seemed at odds with the way her *L'inar* had rippled while watching some of the guards sparring in the gym. Possibly she just found him dull, his thoughts uninspiring. It was a little depressing. Maybe it was because all he had done was fantasize. A fighter like her would probably prefer a man of action.

He stroked himself harder, imagining taking her against the wall in the conference room, or spreading her on the large meeting table so he could lick every inch of her, explore those remarkable nerve lines the Inarrii had on most of their body. Reports were clear on the function of the nerve lines—they controlled the Inarrii's sexuality and reacted to pain and alarm as well. But not everything was laid out in the reports. Why did the lines not extend to her toes?

She had beautiful feet. She wore her shipsuit at all times, not slipping into the comfortable clothes most people wore in their quarters, or any of the traditional Inarrii clothing he'd read about. But one thing she did do when she was relaxed was to remove her ship boots and spread her naked toes on the soft carpets of their common sitting room. The sight of her skin, a golden hue even on the underside of her feet, drove him crazy. He licked his lips as the thick muscle of his cock jerked under his touch.

He'd never fantasized about any woman for this long without making a move. Not that he didn't have lovers, but he kept his relationships short, uninvolved. His work didn't allow him the luxury of a lover to come home to. If anyone discovered he had ties to someone, that person could be in danger. It was the nature of the Starforce Agency. But Sarina was a professional and from the looks of things, she could take care of herself. Not that he was interested in anything long-term. But she presented a seductive challenge, in every sense.

With a groan, he threw off the tangled sheet and rolled out of bed. Sleep wasn't working and the thought of jerking off alone, again, wasn't satisfying. His balls ached from unspent desire. A cool drink was in order. Maybe a beer or two. Not enough to lose his edge; he'd be on duty until this thing was over and the agreement signed. But he needed something to mellow out with before he went crazy and took another walk on the outer skin of the ship just for the hell of it.

He padded to the door leading from his private sleep-room to the common room and slid it open as silently as possible. No need to wake Sarina. If she could sleep through his sexual fantasies— A sudden thought had him stalled in his tracks. Perhaps she *was* sleeping through them, even dreaming while he was thinking of pumping his cock into her until they both screamed. Perhaps his fantasies were adding a little spice to her dreams. He grinned in the darkness of the common room. *Hope she enjoyed the one about the chocolate pudding.*

Shaking his head at his obviously sleep-deprived thoughts, he headed for the small cooling unit. He'd heard the Inarrii had technology that allowed them to dial a number and materialize the food they wanted, but he was satisfied with having a cooler big enough to store a few drinks and treats in his room. Plenty of his past missions didn't have any kind of amenity. As far as this went, at least he had a private bath, a cooler and a soft place to rest at night, even if he wasn't actually sleeping.

He pulled a beer from the cooler and popped the top. He took a long swig, nearly choking as a voice spoke into the darkness around him.

"You're awake."

He took a gulp of air around the cough that threatened to drown him in his drink. "Yeah, I am. Why are you awake?"

"I am awake *because* you are. That's my job, remember?"

He could see her now, barely, a figure sitting on the dark corner of the couch, her feet tucked underneath her. *How long has she been there?* The thought nagged at him. Had she been unable to sleep because of his fantasy?

An edge of guilt sawed at his gut. She hadn't welcomed any advances, but then he hadn't made any. He'd just thought about her, fantasized about her. But if she could feel his desire… Unease tightened his shoulders. His earlier hope that she'd enjoyed his fantasies suddenly felt wrong, like forcing himself on an unwilling partner. This wasn't in his mission briefing, and it was trickier etiquette than the Treaty negotiations he'd been set to guard.

HE WAS BACKING OUT. She could sense him, had been able to feel nothing *but* him for the last hour as he tossed and turned in the sleeproom across from hers. She'd had enough. When she'd heard him step outside his door and into the public area, the ache in her *sinaa* had guided her out after him, even more than her need to fulfill her guard duty. Somewhere in the dark of the human sleep cycle she'd given up on the pretense of rest, and on the urge to keep her hands off this strange alien. He drew her, his sensual fantasies and muscular body giving her hope that she hadn't had in months. Even his foreignness reassured her in an odd way. *He's human; he can't expect the completion of L'inar. He can't miss what he's never experienced.*

But he was drawing back from her now, the same way the Inarrii warriors in her clan had pulled away when they discovered her *L'inar* would never heal.

Her throat ached as humiliation tightened her muscles enough that she could barely swallow the hurt. Anger quickly replaced the anguish. She wasn't going to keep being dismissed. Not like this, and by a human.

She reached for the control on the small table by the couch and toggled the seating light to its lowest setting. Human vision wasn't as acute as Inarrii. The dim light at the base of the couch illuminated the bottom half of the seating unit but left her face in shadows. She stretched out on the couch, her pose deceptively relaxed, and by the way his eyes tracked her movements, he wasn't as disinterested as he pretended. *Not that anyone could be after picturing us in so many couplings.* She smiled. He couldn't see her expression in the dim lighting but she imagined the predatory curl of her lips might be enough to warn him if he had any foresight.

"I'm also awake because you've been lusting so loudly I thought I must either fuck you or smother you with your pillow. Either way, you would be out of your misery and I might get some sleep."

In the silence that followed her statement she could hear his breath as he strained to take enough air into his lungs. *Oh yes, you can't back away from me now, can you?*

"I'm—"

"Don't say you're sorry. Inarrii don't lie, and we don't like dishonesty." She stretched again and felt the heat in his thoughts spark hotter as he finally realized she wore only a *pettan,* the short, loose-wrapped garment covering her only from waist to knee. Her bare breasts peaked under his sharpened scrutiny and a hum of pleasure tingled in the *L'inar* closest to her nipples.

She watched him swallow and carefully set the beer

down on the counter. Inarrii eyesight illuminated the nearly black room to her senses, allowing her to see in glorious detail his thick, jutting cock. He'd forgotten his nudity—humans seemed to have strict taboos about their clothing or lack thereof—but his exposure revealed more to her than his immediate response.

He was as beautifully muscled as she'd imagined. *Not the body of a data tech.* Not the body of an Inarrii warrior either. John Bennings didn't have the density of an Inarrii, but the overall effect of lean muscles, thicker cock, silken body hair and exotic, unmarked skin appealed to her. She licked her lips. *What would he taste like?* His scent still reminded her of the seashore at home, and an image of him lapping at her *sinaa* like the warm sea waves against the shoreline wrapped around her mind, salty sweet. Her *L'inar* ridged around her breasts as she imagined what the sensation would be like, his smooth skin against her. She held back a sigh as her rising nerve endings sent a quick wave of pleasure though her, only slightly marred in its pathway by the disruption in her scarred arm.

His body continued to react to her. She could see the pulse in his neck beating harder. In reaction she slid one hand along the waist of her *pettan*, dipping her fingers inside the edge. He held still, apparently captured by the image she presented, but his cock bobbed as if she'd stroked it instead of her own skin. The contrast confused her. Why did he wait? He wanted her; she'd offered him release. But he stood still.

"Come here." Her voice sounded odd to her. Did it sound strange to him as well? *Be in control.* "Come here and touch me." She considered the feeling of guilt that had infused his earlier emotion when he'd realized he might be keeping her awake. "I can't go back to sleep now."

He took a step closer, two, then seemed to realize how his cock hung there, pointing out his desire. A flush of color stained his cheekbones. *Another human reaction. Delightful.* His embarrassment was touching, but also a lure to her warrior self, one she wanted to pursue. But he was hesitating again. He wanted her. Her *m'ittar* might not tell her his exact thoughts, but he saw her as a viable, desirable bed partner. She'd blatantly invited him to have sex with her, so why did he continue to waver? This was not what usually happened between consenting Inarrii. Sex was either a yes or not now arrangement unless one was permanently mated. Perhaps there was some sort of human cultural condition that made this kind of pairing unacceptable.

She stopped touching herself and stood. "My apologies if I misunderstood your desire. If this is against your custom, please understand that Inarrii don't take offense at rejection. It won't affect our working relationship." She took a step toward her room, but it was also a step toward him.

Her movement seemed to trigger something within him and he reached out and gently caught her upper arm just as she would have passed by him. She sucked in a quick breath as she looked into his eyes and saw naked lust there. Her *L'inar* rippled at the touch of his cool skin against hers where he'd caught her uninjured arm. Pleasure shot through her. When he pulled her against him she let him, allowed him to crush her breasts against his chest. Ripples of pleasure became waves as he wrapped his arms around her, stroked her back. She lost herself to the sensation and murmured approval when his lips touched hers.

Images from his mind assailed her. She'd been right— he, like several of the humans involved in the Treaty, had a form of *m'ittar*, enough to make him doubly attractive. His lust dominated his thoughts. Deliciously dark, heavy with need, his mind kissed her *m'ittar* in a psychic echo of his lips against hers. His thick cock pressed against her *pettan*, seeking a way past the folds of material to reach her heat. She grabbed the muscular lobes of his ass and ground against him. It had been too long, and she wanted this, a wild coupling to heat the blood and leave her gasping for air, even if it wouldn't leave her completely satisfied. She tilted her head away from his, leaned in to nip at his shoulder.

With a growl, he grabbed her around the waist, lifting her until her feet left the floor. She wrapped her legs around his hips in an attempt to grind closer to him. She bit him again, bringing a flush of heat to his shoulder. The slightly salty taste of his skin captured her until a ripple of sexual reaction in her damaged *L'inar* sent wild, uncontrolled sensations down her back. In a quick move he pulled her back to the couch and dropped down on it with her, pinning her beneath him. Surprise, and the heavy weight of his body, brought a gasp to her lips.

He palmed her breast, teased her taut nipple. The fact that he skipped over the *L'inar* that would have been the focus of an Inarrii male's attention and pinched her tender nipple directly made her cry out. Pleasure roared in her ears with every heartbeat. She twisted under him, excited, confused, driven by the desire to rip off her *pettan* and mate, to urge him to pound his cock into her *sinaa*. His need appeared to match hers, and for an instant she wondered if her *m'ittar* was pulling his sensations into her mind and meshing them with her own, or forcing her desire into his mind. She didn't care, couldn't, as she realized he was working his hand into the band of the *pettan* and past the curve of her hips.

In his urgency to reach her, the material began to rip. A bubble of laughter caught in her throat, the insanity of the moment catching and amusing her as nothing had since she'd been injured. She shook her head and yanked at the tie to the clothing, pulling it open before he could ruin it. The closure gave away immediately, cooperating before she would have ripped it open herself. John's strong fingers found her, cupped her and stroked the wet lips of her *sinaa*. His lips met hers and his tongue pushed into her mouth just as his fingers slid inside her.

His nimble fingers teased her, his thumb caressing the ridges of her innermost *L'inar* with each thrust of his fingers into her wet heat. Lines of sensation raced through her, her ridges peaking along her thighs, hips and waist. She groaned as he levered onto his elbow, freeing his other hand just enough to pinch her other nipple with a hard twist. The slight pain ignited her sensory ridges from her breast to her shoulder, pushing pleasure through her. Lightning fast, her *L'inar* stiffened under his caress, and when he pulled his mouth from hers to lick up the side of her neck the connection whipped though her. She bucked, and he thrust his fingers faster into her. A moan shuddered through her—*almost*—she was almost—

With a growl he released her, pulled away and kneeled, only to pick her up as though she weighed nothing and turn her in his arms until her back was pressed against the cool skin of his chest. His breath caressed the *L'inar* on the back of her neck, rewarding her for the loss of the intense spiral she'd been on. With a wordless demand he pulled her down onto his cock from behind, his unusual width parting her, thrusting deep into her.

His cock pumped into her and he cupped her breasts, pulling them forward slightly. He stretched her nipples out until they ached and she leaned forward into the pull. Her *L'inar* ridged and flattened uncontrollably, the sensation flushing heat though her until she began to hope, began to spiral once again. The wildness of the act, the fast, impossible pace as he took her, left her gasping, was unlike anything she'd felt even with the finest Inarrii warrior. The tenderness in her breasts accented the glory in her *sinaa* in a way that almost made her wish for more. John ignored all the usual triggers for her arousal, yet she was torn apart with need and sensation, even elation. *This just might work.*

"John." The word rasped out between her breaths, the first time she'd called him by his name, not his formal surname. "Harder."

DRUNK. He must be drunk, must have had a dozen beers rather than the few swallows he'd downed before she called him to her and bewitched him. Must have, because he couldn't control what he was doing, the way he was taking her without even a little foreplay or a few sensitive words. He just wanted to fuck her like there was never going to be another day. There was only this one moment to mark her, to make her his in a way she'd never forget. So he must be drunk, or crazy. Because she couldn't be his, should not even be in his arms right now.

But she was and he could only focus on her intense reaction, her shuddering gasps and the thin ridges on her back that rippled up and down in waves as he plunged into her tight pussy. She moaned as she rode him, caught up in a chain reaction. He released one of her nipples to stroke the stiffening ridges on her belly and then lower, where several lines twisted and met at the wet edge of her pussy. He pulled all the way out of her so he could have the sensation of penetrating her again. He wasn't going to be able to keep this up. He was losing control, and as amazing as she felt, she wasn't ready to join him. He could feel that, somewhere in the sexual mesh of their minds. He strained to hold back and rubbed her ridges, slowing his plunge and sliding his fingers into her wet well on the offbeats of his thrusts. She responded so strongly he could almost feel her pleasure, could almost imagine burning lines of sensation along his body matching the pattern of her *L'inar*.

He almost didn't hear the first rocking boom. But the second impact threw off his rhythm, and the noise was too loud to ignore. A third blast, as he recognized what it was in his sex-drenched euphoria, slammed through the outer bulkhead. A chunk of the wall flew forward and ripped into the room. He twisted, slid down to the floor, sheltered her body with his. *Of all the time for an attack…* A shearing pain in his back left him gasping for air.

"The ship is under attack. We have to get out of here!" Her voice seemed muffled. She twisted away from him.

He made a grab for her, tried to keep her from moving from the little shelter he could offer her. "Sarina." It seemed hard to get her name past his lips.

Something wasn't right. The ship was under attack. Another blast of laser fire slammed into the wall. She was moving away from him, and he tried to pull her back.

"You're wounded. We must get you to the medtechs," she told him. Her voice seemed far away, echoing like a distorted vid. Her face was close to his again. Agony roared through him with each breath and he looked down at his chest. Blood rushed from the edges of a rough piece of metal that pierced his skin. He was run through, he realized, skewered by a part of the bulkhead. The outer wall must have pushed through the inner.

"They are shooting at this section and the shields are giving," she shouted at him over the sound of more impacts. "If we don't move, the air is going to get sucked out of here when the shields die." She stared at him.

He knew what she was thinking. He was going into shock. She was right.

"I'm sorry."

Before he had a chance to imagine what she might be sorry for, she stood and hauled him to his feet. Pain burned white-hot, and he cried out as the metal piercing him was ripped from his chest. When his knees buckled she grabbed him in a rough hold, taking his weight easily. As the room blackened around him he realized she was carrying him, her slight frame supporting his completely as she dragged him from the room.

Chapter 3

"The attack was definitely centered on your sector of the ship. No other area took any major damage."

Sarina nodded. Commander Jannii Finar, commander of the Jupiter Moon Inarrii outbase, grimaced over the vid channel as he watched her strap on the last of her *dash'tet*. She hadn't thought she would need them on this assignment. In truth, she'd thought she would never have need of the warrior knives ever again. She wondered if Finar had thought the same. Finar was one of the few who had never commented on her injury one way or the other—never given her the false platitudes or the flat-out dismissal of her abilities once it became clear the medtechs couldn't completely heal her. There was no way to reattach *L'inar* that had been severed completely from the central column.

Now the knives offered a familiar weight on her forearms. She was dressed for war once again. Knives, spikes, lasers and the nearly indestructible perma-plas uniform, the same as she had worn a hundred times before. Wearing them again and reviewing mission details in her native tongue, rather than the complicated human language, was both a relief and a concern. "The attack seems to have been unusually pinpointed."

"Agreed. John Bennings was the only possible target.

31

All other legal personnel were located in the seventh section, basically the other end of the ship. The *Osprey* itself was the only ship in this sector under attack."

"Why would Bennings be the target? He is hardly a major component for the completion of the Treaty. He is only a lawyer."

Finar hesitated then responded with a negating motion of his hands—the Inarrii equivalent of a human shrug. "It is possible he was targeted *because* he was the only legal personnel in that area."

Sarina tugged an extra laser harness over her chest. Overkill perhaps, considering the man she was supposed to be protecting wouldn't be going anywhere for a little while. Safely ensconced in an Inarrii medlab on a docked shuttle inside the human's *SS Osprey*, John would be unconscious for the next few hours at least. His injury had been severe, far worse than hers had been. He'd almost died.

"Not likely. If they had struck where the other personnel were located, the likelihood of them eliminating more than one target in the attack would have been much higher. Was there anything else in that sector, maybe something we were not aware of? I did an initial sweep upon arrival and sector two appeared the most protected. I moved us there but did not identify any other potential target. It is probably what saved John's life."

"You are developing a relationship with Bennings." It wasn't a question. Inarrii warriors were expected to form attachments and even sexual relationships with the people they protected. It made the desire to protect much stronger and was a logical product of long periods of time alone together.

"Simple sex." Sarina turned her attention to the set of her chest holster. A perfect fit could mean the difference between life and death.

"I would suggest some caution in this, Tariim. Humans do not really have simple sex. And your condition—"

"My condition is under control. And it has nothing to

do with the current situation, sir." Sarina didn't look at the screen. Although they were not friends, his tone was personal. It would have hurt to see him wear an expression of doubt, or worse, pity.

"Very well. Have you noticed anything about Bennings that might indicate a reason for him being the target?"

Images of John's muscular body flickered though her mind. He moved with the same grace as a trained warrior. That was what seemed so familiar about him. He reminded her of the bunkmate she'd had on her fourth mission against the Archats, an Inarrii warrior who'd died without sending a single message to his clan. He'd been a loner, just as John appeared to be. She had not seen John participate in any social discussions. Perhaps that was the only true similarity.

"No. Nothing. He completes the work assigned to him but doesn't show any particular importance."

"At this time we are breaking up the human legal team to relocate them on board the Horneu. Bennings will be the last to move out, as he is still under medical care. You will have the Inarrii medtech shuttle at your command and an escort of two fighters."

"Understood."

"Be careful, *Soryen* Tariim. I'll see you on board the Horneu. *Tel sahiir denay.*"

Sarina nodded and flicked the vid panel off. There was nothing to do now but wait. She replayed the conversation with Finar as she made a final check of her equipment. The canny commander obviously suspected something was off about John Bennings. And he might be right.

Sarina glanced around the compartment. A makeshift patch covered the damage to the hull wall. Her belongings and those of her charge had already been packed up and would now be shifted to the shuttle. Her eyes lingered on the couch. She licked her lips, felt a stirring in the unreliable lines of her *L'inar*. Something had happened between them, more than the casual sex she'd admitted to Finar.

She'd felt the first brush of true *m'ittar* mind contact between them. More, she'd felt her *L'inar* respond in a way she'd no longer thought possible. Not that she expected she could have achieved full release. That was too much to hope for. But there had been something. She strode to the door and out into the main corridor. There might not be anything more to do but wait, but she was going to be there when John regained consciousness.

She might have let her clan down, might never bring them another honor point, but she wasn't about to leave her charge unprotected. That tiny brush of hope she felt within her in his embrace reminded her just how far she'd fallen. What kind of a warrior was she now; what kind of female had she become? The thought hit her like a blow. She straightened her shoulders. Desperation was not a mindset she'd ever accepted. Besides, she had questions for the man and they had unfinished business.

Sarina walked through the human ship, quietly assessing the damage from the recent attack as she worked her way toward the Inarrii shuttle. Commander Finar was correct. Their sector was the only one to take any note-worthy hits from the fighter ships. She scanned the codes on the walls that identified the sector, level and use of each room she passed. Unlike the visually stimulating pictographs and glowing controls commonly used by the Inarrii, human identity codes were simple, and not terribly descriptive. But then, humans didn't have the visual scope of Inarrii, couldn't see the same spectrum of light. Without entering the rooms, she couldn't be certain the human tags were even correct. But her initial explorations and those she had completed over the last three days indicated they were, and that there was nothing to offer a target to the terrorists or the alien Ravagers.

It all came down to John Bennings. Someone in the terrorist group wanted him, *specifically*, dead.

The Inarrii medical shuttle had docked inside the landing bay of sector four. The *Osprey* was laid out in fairly logical order, at least to her mind. Perhaps it was because she was a warrior and this was a human military ship, but it seemed as though the humans and the Inarrii had more in common than their physical shape. She considered the similarities of John's muscular body. True, he had no *L'inar*, but he was attractive to her. His long legs and wide shoulders drew her, and the light covering of hair in various spots on his body was oddly pleasant to touch.

Even his *m'ittar* seemed different, alien, yet close enough for her to merge with his pleasure and he with hers. She'd felt more with him than she'd expected to. But then, she'd had no physical contact since her injury with anyone other than Examiner Salis Fiiten, who had acted as her therapist since her injury. Much as she'd tried, she couldn't find release with the therapist. He'd tried his best, but her *L'inar* were ruined and he, well, something was different with the Examiner. He had a distance within him that she'd thought was a reaction to her injury. Now she wondered if that was true. He seemed unable to open part of his mind to their pleasure. Perhaps it was simply that he was an Examiner, not a true therapist. He had the memories of a hundred cases in his mind, many things that would be impossible share, even on a subliminal level. Or perhaps he had just been unable to respond to someone with damaged *L'inar*, even if he had wanted to for her sake.

Sarina rounded the corner to the shuttle dock and paused in front of the scanner until it recognized her DNA. Walking through the hatch, she nodded to the Inarrii fighter pilots lounging in the reception center. They barely acknowledged her, but that was probably because of the lively three-dimensional *haisto* game they had running on the vid. *Haisto* seemed to take up the spare time of every pilot she knew—the live adaption of human poker and chess combined with war strategy developed by the first surveillance team in their off time had quickly become the perfect pastime for the flying warrior clans.

She walked by and palmed the glowing control to the doors of the medlab.

"*Soryen Tariim. Inar tel sahiir.*" The healer greeted her through the mind contact of *m'ittar* as she entered.

"*Inar tel sahiir, Medtech Yassin.*" She returned the formal greeting. Between the warrior clans there was no need for formality, but she wasn't familiar with the clan of this healer. Being impolite could, at very least, slow her mission.

"*You are the warrior with the severed L'inar.*" It wasn't a question. It seemed as though every medtech on the mission had been exposed to her case. "*I have been experimenting with electro impulse conductive gel—*"

"*Very interesting. Perhaps we can discuss that later. How is your patient?*" She brought the discussion back to where it should be, focused on the status of her charge and how long they would have to wait before they could move out. She'd heard too many pet theories on nerve reconnection.

Taking the hint, the medtech moved to the control panel beside the medbed. He brought up a scan of the lawyer's healing injuries. Sarina glanced at the brightly patterned vid and then looked down at the bed. John's body lay on the surface, entirely covered in the *dorii-chiksin* —a woven cover of sensors and microthin tools able to penetrate a patient's skin and access the inner organs and tissue without pain. She could see nothing of the patient inside, since the *dorii* covered him like a cocoon, but that was typical and not alarming. She had to wonder if John would feel the same way. She knew from experience waking inside the *dorii* could be disturbing. Coming to in darkness, immobilized and bound, if loosely, was always a shock.

"*John Bennings is nearly healed.*"

"*When will he be able to move? A second attack is more than likely. It would be best if we could be in a more protected position.*" Sarina resisted the urge to touch the figure on the medbed.

"*The recent damage has already been repaired. However, the older scar tissue will take some time to remove.*"

Sarina glanced at the technician. "*Older scar tissue?*" She kept her mental voice casual, but an image of the way John moved with a warrior's grace flashed into her thoughts. Quickly she strengthened the shields around her mind. No need to raise her suspicions when they were only that.

"*He has multiple areas of layered scar tissue beneath the top layer of skin.*" The healer shook his head. "*The humans will be happy to receive our healing technology. If this is the best they can do with laser burns, I pity their patients. The healing he has received for most of his older injuries has been purely cosmetic.*"

The healer pointed to a long white mark on the display vid of John's body. Scar tissue. She scanned the display more carefully. John had many of what appeared to be old injuries. Not what one would expect from a lawyer. She hadn't noticed anything the previous evening. It might have only been cosmetic, but the work done had been excellent camouflage.

"*Leave the scars for now. We need to move out, away from the Osprey, and get to the Horneu.*"

The medtech waved his hands, his feelings about leaving the healing incomplete clear through their light *m'ittar* contact. But he complied, applying a thin line of laser against the *dorii-chiksin*. Sarina watched as the folds of medical cloth released and separated, folding back and revealing the man underneath. Light brown hair, cleansed by the same microthin tools in the *dorii* that would have dealt with body waste, seemed wavy rather than spiked as she remembered. It looked softer to the touch, something she would enjoy taking her time exploring. In seconds his face, still relaxed in unconsciousness, emerged. He had more body hair on his face than before, a thin layer of darker color. Idly she wondered if it would feel soft as well.

Slowly the human's athletic frame was revealed. Wide, thickly muscled shoulders and a chest with deeply outlined pectorals raised a quick flair of interest across the *L'inar* on the back of her neck and across her breasts. She was grateful her fighting gear and uniform covered her reaction, as she had no desire to have the medtech insist on observing how her sensory lines reacted in a case of actual stimulation. Instead she concentrated on the human before her.

A small amount of light brown curls nestled in the center of his chest and faded down into a silky line that almost reached his navel. She remembered the feel of them, crisp yet silky at the same time. Slowly the layers of the *dorii* peeled away from his underbelly. She sucked in a breath as she saw the sleek line of hair begin again, pointed downward and widening slightly, an arrow of decoration that was as attractive as any *L'inar* swirl pattern. She'd missed that pattern in their first frenzied encounter. Her fingers itched to touch, and her sensory nerve lines crested along the edges of her breasts in response to the vision presented before her.

"Ahem."

Sarina glanced at John's face to find him watching her. His eyes were dark, the pupils wide. Her *L'inar* flickered with a rapid intensity. The uniform she'd been glad for moments earlier suddenly felt tight, hot.

"You're awake." Sarina took a step toward the head of the bed.

The medtech silently continued his work, releasing the rest of the *dorii* from John's body.

"You are in an Inarrii medical laboratory. You were injured in a terrorist attack against the *Osprey*. We have healed your injuries. You will be released from care in a few minutes. All legal personnel are being relocated to the Inarrii flagship, the Horneu."

John brushed aside the last loose remnants of the *dorii* from his arm and lifted a hand to touch his chest where he'd been wounded. "How long have I been under?"

"Only about fourteen of your earth hours, not yet a full day."

"You should remain in medical care for some time longer," the medtech interjected. "We could remove all the old scar tissue from your previous injuries." The Inarrii healer was working to release John's calves.

Both John and Sarina glanced down at the medtech, but Sarina's gaze was snagged as she caught sight of John's cock, naked and half-hard. She pulled her gaze away, looked back at his face.

If she hadn't glanced back at that moment, Sarina would have missed the slight thinning of John's lips as he pressed them tightly together and the fleeting dark expression, almost anger, on his face as he stared at the healer. "No, thanks. If we've been attacked once, we might be attacked again, and I don't want to hold up the evacuation."

"The evacuation has already begun. You will actually be the last to move out," Sarina stated and turned to glance at the monitoring vid. It was safer than looking at the curve of muscle under John's skin. "But you are correct. It is best if we move quickly."

John flexed and then swung his legs over the edge of the medical bed as he sat up. "Let's go now. I need to complete…" He touched his forehead as a wave of apparent dizziness hit him. "My assignment…"

———

SHADOWS LURKED at the edges of his vision. Sarina grabbed his elbow and steadied him, her strong fingers wrapped securely around his elbow. *Bloody hell.* He must have been more injured than he'd thought, or this healing thing took more out of a person than he imagined. He'd come perilously close to saying something he shouldn't have, an error he'd never committed in ten years of high-level missions. And Sarina smelled so good, looked so good in her layers of weaponry. It had to be the sexiest outfit he'd ever seen.

"I have to get back to the others and finish the agreement," he said. "We clearly need it more than ever."

Sarina was watching him, but she gave a small, slow nod. She was buying it. *Maybe.*

"Were any of the others injured?"

"No. Only you. Only our sector received any damage." She met his eyes. She suspected something, no doubt about it. And if he'd been the only member of the legal team injured, it would probably appear that he was the target. He was supposed to be a nonentity, a nobody lawyer. Someone out there must be aware of his cover. It was the only possibility.

"You are free to go, although I am noting that it is against my recommendation." The medtech passed him a *pettan*. John eyed the short covering. He wasn't even sure how to put the damn thing on, but he didn't want to walk around naked either.

"Do you require assistance?" Sarina might suspect him, but she was amused. And possibly still sexually interested, considering the tiny raised edge of her *L'inar* that he could see near the collar of her uniform. It was an angle that just might put her suspicion on hold. Plus, a more sexual approach to his cover, considering the way she'd felt in his arms last night, would be very satisfying all around.

He pretended to growl at her, but he flexed slightly as he put one leg into the *pettan*. *Go ahead and look, sweetie.* He considered trying to project a sexual thought toward her, but a slight sound from the medtech reminded him he had more than one person in the audience, so to speak. And considering the way the Inarrii male was looking at them, he might be hoping for an invitation, something John wasn't prepared to offer.

Hurriedly he pulled the *pettan* on and struggled to tie the closure. After a moment Sarina stepped forward and pulled the ties from his hands. She made quick work of them, but John's breath caught as she brushed against his thigh, and the material snagged lightly against the skin of his cock. The unexpected gesture was so intimate he sucked in a quick breath of air. Despite the clinical tang of the medlab he could smell her hair, the clean scent that was her skin. Clearly he was recovering quickly from the Inarrii healing because if they didn't get somewhere private soon, he might make her an offer, audience be damned.

"Medtech Yassin, you are relieved of duty. This shuttle is now under my command." Her voice was cool as she addressed the technician; perhaps she wasn't as affected by the act of binding him as he was.

John took another breath and moved aside. Control—he needed it now.

"Very well. Perhaps we will meet again and discuss your injury and possible treatment." For an instant John was confused as to whom the man was talking to, and then he realized the medtech was speaking to Sarina.

He glanced at her. Had she been injured in the attack as well? If she had, it wasn't evident. Were her old injuries still bothering her? Because she sure as hell didn't move like they were.

"Another time, Medtech Yassin. *Tel sahür denay.*" Sarina headed for the door.

John followed a few steps behind, giving the medical technician a nod and a smile.

"*Inar choksan,*" Sarina spoke to the two Inarrii in the exterior room.

They snapped off the vid game they had been playing and rose to attention. John hid a grin at the note of command in her voice. *Damn, she's sexy when she's the boss.* It gave him some entirely inappropriate ideas when he should be working out how to contact his mission tech. He was relieved when she continued in his own language. Beyond a few common phrases and commands, the Inarrii language was one he had yet to master.

"Take your positions. We are heading for the Horneu

within the hour, once the medical personnel moves off board and we are given permission to take off."

The nearest pilot nodded. "Good flying, Tariim. There have been no reported attacks on the other evacuees."

"Well, let's hope that continues to be the case and we are ignored as well. We have the medical markings on the shuttle to offer us some anonymity."

The pilot waved his hands in an Inarrii shrug and turned away. She stared after them as they headed for the shuttle bay hatch. John watched her. Despite her attentive gaze she seemed lost in her thoughts.

When she stepped forward again, turning right and walking through a corridor hatch, John followed once again. Tagging along was beginning to feel a little stale. He needed information. A quick scan of the common area before they left offered him an option—there was a communications panel in one corner. All he needed was a few moments of privacy and he could be in touch with Davis. No doubt the man knew of John's injury and his eventual transport. But what Davis was aware of could also be common knowledge for whoever had pinned him in the first place.

Sarina stopped in the next room, only a few feet away from what must be the shuttle's command center and three curved seats. It took him a second to catch his momentum, his thoughts centering on contacting his Starforce mission tech. He came close to her, nearly brushing up against her. When she turned toward him, he was close enough to touch his lips to hers, but the look in her eyes told him this would not be the best idea.

"So, John Bennings, what kind of lawyer is covered in laser scars, moves like a warrior born and is singled out for a Ravener attack when there are bigger, juicier targets all around?"

Chapter 4

Sarina studied John's expression. His face had gone blank as she'd begun to question him. There were no clues to his feelings. His thoughts were also tightly shuttered. That in itself seemed odd; for a man whose sexual fantasies were projected loud and clear, his general thoughts appeared highly contained. Finally he took a step away and turned to sit in one of the command console chairs. She let him have a moment, but kept her stance balanced. Inarrii rarely lied since it went against their beliefs and the natural honesty inspired by *m'ittar,* but she knew very well that many other species had the ability to avoid the truth.

"The scars—" He hesitated and then began again, his eyes downcast. "The scars I got from a serious industrial accident several years ago, when I was only twenty. I was pretty stupid. Thought I was invincible. They were painful and looked terrible. I had them altered so I could look as normal as possible." He looked up at her and smiled, but the expression didn't meet his eyes. "They did a good job. I took up karate, what we call a martial art, as a way to recover. It acted as a kind of therapy to deal with the injury and get stronger.

"As for the Raveners, I have no idea why they seem to

have attacked me in particular. I am only one in a team of people acting on Earth's behalf."

He stared at her. She searched his eyes and extended her *m'ittar*. It was a breach of etiquette, but she didn't push too hard. Nothing. He remained blank to her. But his story seemed to hold a hint of truth, at least to her ears. He'd explained everything very neatly, except his part as target for the Raveners. Who could say what their motive was? They had somehow homed in on him, but that could still be coincidence. She would confirm his story about being injured years ago, but the reflected hurt in his eyes matched the scans of the scars on his body. He really had experienced agony and overcome it. Perhaps this was one thing they had in common.

"I was injured, as you may know, on the Horneu in the last major terrorist attack. My arm was nearly severed." She offered the commonality and waited. This was the point when an Inarrii would link the events, realize she had lost her *L'inar* connections and pull away from her.

Instead, the human nodded in commiseration. "I'm sorry you had that kind of pain. It's good that your technology has allowed you to recover completely." His eyes held some sympathy, but at least it was only from the thought of the agony she had endured. He didn't know the rest.

"I am not healed, not entirely. A large section of my *L'inar* was severed from the central nervous column. They cannot be repaired." She heard her own voice calmly tell him what any Inarrii would understand to be the end of her career, if not her life. She knew he wouldn't understand the ramifications, wouldn't look at her with horror and pity. But still, the words were difficult to say aloud. She thought of the flash of hope she'd felt in his arms as he drove them both toward a peak she'd thought never to see again.

He watched her, waited for her to say something more.

Sarina debated with herself. There was still something

very different about this man. Perhaps it was because he was human. The circumstances they found themselves in certainly had been layered with a tension that made trusting him difficult. But she found him appealing, his strength and sexuality an attractive balm to her damaged senses. If he could truly bring her to orgasm, then she had something she could hope for.

"I would like to continue where we left off before you were injured, if you are interested. If you were Inarrii, I would not need to be so direct, but I am not certain of your customs. I would like to have sex with you, many times, to see if we can stimulate my *L'inar* as we did the other night in a sustainable way." She plunged through the words in a headlong gallop, like a wild *yimnar* on the sand dunes of her home world. Immediately she regretted the request. Now wasn't the time. Their earlier experience was acceptable in relation to her duty—connection to her charge was good and there had been no indication of danger at that time.

Now, his life was at risk. Sex was a relief, but it could also be a distraction.

Guilt bit at her. What if he was injured again? What if she lost her concentration on his safety during a sexual affair? And on another level, her embarrassment ranked nearly as highly as her guilt. She'd never had to ask for sex; as a high-ranking warrior from one of the most honorable clans, she'd always been the one sought after. Now her clan had abandoned her and she'd resorted to soliciting humans.

Surprise filtered over his face. Clearly she had startled him, but he didn't look offended. His eyes darkened; his skin flushed. The nipple buds on his chest tightened in what she knew was human sexual reaction. Watching him sent a wave of interest through the *L'inar* along her scalp, down the center of her back.

When he stood, his once-blank *m'ittar* flared, a quick flame of lust that singed her mind.

"Sergeant Tariim, Medship Five, Medtech Yassin is off board and you are cleared for take off." The voice of the *Osprey's* human commtech cut into the moment, slicing it as cleanly as a warrior's *dash'tet*.

Sarina stifled a groan and chided herself. This was not the time for pleasure or therapy of any kind. She had her duty—to get her charge to the Horneu safely, no matter what his past was or what he could offer her. He must complete his part of the Treaty. "*Inar sho sahiir*, Osprey, this is Medship Five," she responded. She felt John's eyes on her and fought the desire to look back at him as she settled into the pilot chair. "Are our escorts fired up?"

"Escorts are making their pass along the ship now, Tariim. You're set. Have a safe journey."

Sarina slid her fingers over the controls. The Inarrii flight panel sprang to life, the color and tones of the light telling her the status of the ship on a subliminal level as well as in literal linear readouts. The hum of ultrasonics filtered through the soles of her boots as they had a thousand times before and she slipped into the comfortable routine of take off. Sonic waves pushed the shuttle gently from the dock and into space. Despite the familiarity of flight, a line of tension snaked through her belly. From here until they reached the Horneu, they would be vulnerable.

The ship reached the safe zone and she kicked in the pulse engine, boosting the shuttle into the first velocity cycle. Curving the direction of the shuttle toward Mars, the two Inarrii fighter escorts entered the edge of the vid screen and took flanking positions to the shuttle.

John sat quietly beside her in the copilot command chair. She could feel the intensity of his gaze even without the contact of *m'ittar* as he watched her every move. She continued her security check and initiated full battle screens. They limited the visual and sensing range of the ship, but the force screens would protect the medship from fairly heavy fire.

After a few minutes John stood and excused himself.

She didn't watch him leave. When in her life had she been so embarrassed? Never. He wanted her, but the whole experience had become awkward, something she hadn't expected.

JOHN GROUND his teeth together as he left the control room. More than anything he would like to take Sarina and tie her to a bed somewhere. Screw her until they'd both had enough and could concentrate on their respective jobs. But that wasn't going to happen. She'd asked him to have sex—lots of sex—and she was already all he could think about. This had to be the worst case of bad timing, ever. He could sense a vulnerability in her when she told him about her injury and yet he had no choice but to use that opening to continue with his mission.

This was the only moment where Sarina was too busy with the ship's controls, and possibly with her own thoughts, to have any time to suspect him or to watch what he was doing. It was the perfect time to set up communications with Davis. He *had* to.

You could have taken the time to say yes, you idiot, he berated himself, but leaving her hanging was the best thing for the mission, wasn't it? He resisted the urge to bang his head against the wall as he found the stash of his personal belongings at the back of the shuttle lounge. All of his things from the Osprey had been packed into two small duffle bags.

He grabbed his wrist comp and slapped it on. Sarina would have to stay at the controls while they made the four-hour trip; at least, that's what a human pilot would do without a backup. John walked over to the communication panel. With a few strokes of command on his wrist unit, he made a connection and inserted the codes for covert mode.

"Davis, up and at 'em." He spoke quietly.

"Well, playboy, good to finally hear from you."

"Hey, I was injured. Where were you when I was in an alien medical lab? You didn't even send flowers." John couldn't resist the quip. For just an instant he felt normal again, in control.

"I would have, but I wasn't sure if your Inarrii girl-friend would approve. Heard she hauled you in naked and bloody. Must have been quite a night."

John pressed his lips together. He had a serious desire to tell Davis to go fuck himself, but that would only encourage the idiot. He glanced down at his writ comp. Data flowed in from Davis. The man might be a jerk at times, but he knew his job and was streaming the latest updates immediately, in case their communication was cut off.

"Back off there, bud. There was no way she could know we'd be attacked. She saved my life."

"Okay. Are you good?"

"Yeah, but I figure someone has me pinned. They have me as an agent, or something. They've been going straight for me."

"Yeah. I know. I'd pull you, but the CIC says stay put and keep at it. She probably thinks you're a better target than the real civilians."

"And she'd be right. We're headed to the Horneu, and I'll maintain cover there."

"Just don't go too deep undercover, bud. I hear sex with those aliens ruins you for human pussy."

Annoyance burned at a spot behind John's eyes. He rubbed his head but kept his reply casual. "Well then, Davis, I'll be clear to hit on you."

Davis killed the line, but not before John heard his snort of derision. A tickle of irritation remained from their conversation. The man could be a real asshole. Maybe he just needed to get laid. He cut the connection between his wrist comp and the communication panel, then turned and stared at the doorway that led to the control room.

He owed Sarina an answer. She'd been honest with

him and he'd done nothing but lie. Davis was right about one thing—getting involved was stupid. But he'd never claimed to be that smart.

SARINA HEARD John step back into the control room. Whatever he'd been doing, it hadn't taken long. He stood behind her, obviously waiting. For the first quarter of the flight she ignored him. Finally she turned back to him. Her *L'inar* nerves rippled erratically, and her heart beat harder. It was irrational—if he refused her, she would be no worse off than she was before. But...if he agreed, she had the prospect of engaging in a sensual exploration with a human male every bit as attractive as any Inarrii warrior she'd ever bunked with, assuming they had time once they reached the Horneu. She tried to shrug it off before she met his eyes. It was possible that even if he agreed they would not be able to find an opportunity. She may even be reassigned once they reached the Horneu, as he was now considered a more important target, and her reputation had already bottomed out.

His gaze met hers. Whatever he'd been doing before, he was waiting for her now to continue, to say something more about her desire for him. She wished she'd been more lyrical, more seductive. But she was warrior clan. They didn't practice the seductive arts—when you wanted sex with a bunkmate, you reached out and laid hands on his *L'inar*. But for the first time in her life she wished for the gentler words. The soft gray of his eyes seemed darker now, more intent. The power of his focus wrung sensation from her damaged nerves and sent a tremor up her spine.

"You want to have sex with me." He spoke first, taking away her chance to forget her request. His voice had deepened, and she resonated with it.

"Yes. You are attractive, and you elicit a response from

my *L'inar.* It could be a…a form of therapy, one we could both enjoy."

"Therapy."

"Yes, like your karate."

"You're comparing the heat we experienced to karate." His voice sounded harsh, perhaps somewhat strangled.

"Is that a problem? Is there an issue with your culture? I enjoyed our coupling. I thought it might be beneficial to try it again."

He turned away to look out the vid screen into the filtered view of space.

Sarina's *L'inar* flattened. He seemed perplexed by her request. It made sense for them to have sex, and it would be, from the taste she'd had earlier, delicious. The man was deeply sexual, at least according to the inventive fantasies he'd broadcast in their first few days on board the Osprey. Even if she didn't have a way with words he must be intrigued with her request. *Unless he found you wanting. You are making an idiot of yourself.*

"Apparently you've put some thought into this."

Sarina opened her mouth to reply, to tell him to forget what she'd said earlier, but a flare of light across the filtered vid screen caught her attention.

John leaned close to the screen. "Laser fire!"

"Medship Five, we are under attack." The voice of the first Inarrii escort pilot called though the communication link.

Sarina scrambled to take in the tactical layout of their position. The human starship Osprey was behind them now; the Medship and its two escorts had just passed the Earth's moon on route to the Inarrii Mars base. The attackers were moving in on a tangent coming from a pocket of space littered with debris. They must have laid in wait, biding their time until the right target approached.

"Terran Purity. They're terrorists." John's voice held a bite of anger.

She glanced over at him. His hands were fisted. There

was nothing he could do—the Inarrii fighters would hold off the attackers or not. Sarina eyed the level of silent fire-play going on in the space field nearest them. The Inarrii were outpowered. The aging human ships had clearly been rigged with advanced Ravener weapons. She flicked her fingers over the minimal weapons layout of the Medship. Medical shuttles didn't come heavily armed; they were meant for maneuverability. She hoped there was some kind of laser—they were going to need it.

"Medship, you had better run for it!" The warning was punctuated with bright bursts of laser fire. The escorts were holding the Raveners off but they weren't going to last. Already their shields were partially down and the Raveners were closing in. Huge laser cannons had been added to the salvaged wrecks of the terrorist ships. The strategist in Sarina wondered if that had been the Gathan's adaptation, or a human idea. Both races had aggressive tendencies, but the Gathan, a cold, blue-skinned race, had newly joined the Ravener side. With those evil pirates it was join or be devoured. They were the ones powering the attacks, not the humans. The humans probably didn't even know they'd paired up with a group that would, in the end, destroy Earth.

"*Tel sho ahoi*, Medship Five SOS." Sarina sent a distress signal to both Inarrii and human channels. "We are under attack." Light flared across the screen in a blinding glare. "*Tel sho ahoi sho amnetii.* Ship down—we have lost our escort." Her fingers danced over the glowing controls, and she sent of a volley of shots toward the attackers. Her small lasers bounced ineffectively against the fighter's shielding.

"We've got to get out of here." John began to fumble with the securing straps on his chair.

"Absolutely." Sarina powered the engines to a higher level, forcing the emergency batteries to spike.

The shuttle pulled away from the firefight and the last

escort fighter followed, breaking off from the smaller attackers.

"Medship Five, I have taken substantial damage." The Inarrii fighter pilot called in, his Inarrii words heavily accented with an emotion and a level of determination she knew too well. Still, she had to offer a way out.

"Pull around to flank us, *sho'tet*. We will outrun them."

"I am unable to obey. It has been an honor. Please pass word of my death to my clan. They should reap a good bit of honor credit. *Tel sahiir denay*."

"*Tel sahiir denay*." Sarina grit her teeth as the Inarrii limped back toward the terrorist ships. If she lived though the attack, she would have to find out his full name and clan affiliation, and that of their other escort.

"What's happening?" John's voice, low and serious sounded beside her.

"The *sho'tet* go to give their lives now so we can escape. They fight to the death."

"They could try to escape—"

"They die honorably."

"You sound like you envy them."

Sarina didn't respond. The fighter dropped back even farther and once again began to fire at the following attack ships. The Inarrii *sho'tet* was ending his life and giving them a chance to escape. It was a positive death. After her injury and drop in status, she could only hope for the same.

Chapter 5

S arina spiked the emergency power again and checked tactical. They were going to have to change strategy—there wasn't much choice. She turned to face her charge. John stared back at her. Tension creased the skin between his eyes as she spoke.

"We cannot out-fire them, and our support is about to be wiped out. No one can reach us from the Osprey or the Horneu in time, and we can only outrun them for another few minutes. Then we are going to run out of power. As I see it, we only have one choice."

"We make ourselves invisible," John stated.

He was too calm. Her own heart was pounding, and he was jumping to the same conclusion that her years of experience knew was their only hope. "Yes. We head for the dark side of your moon, disappear in a crater."

His eyes searched hers. He had something to say but he was hesitating.

She opened her *m'ittar* but he remained tightly shut against her.

"I understand there was an Inarrii surveillance base somewhere on the moon," he offered. "Can we use it?" He looked away from her for a second. When he glanced back his jaw was clenched. "I read some reports that I had no legitimate access to. But I did read them. Can we use the base?"

"Yes." She put the plan in motion. It didn't matter how he knew; they needed a way out of this disaster and his idea was a good one, something she hadn't even thought of.

Firing another blast of power to the engines, she made a sharp turn back toward the earth's moon. In the corner of the vid screen the flashing shots of laser fire continued. They had minutes to find a location before the terrorists would be on them again. John stayed silent as she set the comp to finding the location. Again and again her gaze leaped back to the battle on the edge of her screen. The *sho'tet* had been damn good. But the Inarrii pilot was dying.

"There—in that series of craters." Sarina spoke to herself as much as to John. His eyes were locked on the screen, his attention on the space battle. As she toggled the controls toward her choice of hiding places, an explosion pulled her attention back to the final act of her Inarrii escort. He'd reached the point where he could not fight and he'd flown directly into one of the terrorist attackers, removing one more of the terrorists from the chase. She bit back an oath as tears welled in her eyes. There was no time to regret an honorable sacrifice; they needed to use the time he had given them to hide.

Sliding the controls to force the shuttle into a sideways spin, Sarina shot the craft down toward the moon's surface. Flying into the crater was tricky, but that was the point. Despite the growing darkness she did not ignite the shuttle's landing lights. Instead, she relied on the craft's external sensors to relay the dimensions of the crater to her through the vid. At the last instant before they would have hit the bottom, she stopped the descent, flicked off the ship's shields and moved forward along the wall of the crater.

Her *L'inar* rippled. If they didn't find the hidden entrance soon, they were dead.

"*Ken stasht*," she swore under her breath. "There you are." A thin break in the wall, at least according to the ship's sensors, appeared along the edge of the crater. They moved forward slowly, following the break until it widened into a tunnel. Sarina edged the shuttle inside until it was as deep within the rock walls. She tapped the glowing control panel before her and put out the landing gear. Then she shut down everything except minimal life support.

FOR ALMOST A MINUTE, they sat in the near darkness. Only a tiny emergency light emitted a pale green glow from under the control panel.

"What the hell just happened?" John broke into the silence. Their Inarrii escort had just consigned himself to death. He knew it, but he didn't know why. It was something he would do himself, if duty called for it. But Sarina sounded almost envious of the man.

"We'll sit here and hope they pass us by. With no power running, as long as we stay silent they shouldn't be able to detect us through the rock." She fingered one of the long knives strapped to the side of her forearm. "The *sho'tet* are literally that—flying blades. He wasn't going to make it with us and might have even slowed us down. He went back to buy us time, and his clan, his family, will earn a level of honor and credit by his actions that would equal an entire lifetime of fighting."

"You sound as though you think he was lucky."

"He was. He could have been wounded and lost his ability to bring honor to his clan. What good is it to live like that?" She pulled off the straps securing her to the command chair. He could barely make her out in the shadows, although she seemed to have no difficulty with the darkness. During the battle, with the vid screen filtered and the flat control panels glowing, he'd been reminded that she truly was an alien. She'd been seeing things he couldn't. Intel reported a different level of visual acuity in the Inarrii, and she'd just confirmed it.

How much more different was their race than he'd thought? Their sense of duty and honor were deeply ingrained, and he couldn't help respecting that. And she was fantastic—cool as ice under fire. She'd kick ass as an agent. She was fucking beautiful.

"So, you enjoyed our coupling." He kept his voice low, quiet even to his own ears. Even an Inarrii would have to listen closely to hear him, to focus on what he was saying.

She jerked slightly in her chair. He couldn't see it, but he heard the whisper of her uniform moving in her surprise. It reminded him that he wore nothing but the *pettan* the medtech had given him. He could feel his cock stiffen slightly as he remembered what Sarina had looked like in a *pettan* on board the Osprey. He imagined she could see him now, with her Inarrii vision. Like a cat, she could see his every movement in the small amount of available light.

"I did. It was…powerful."

"And if I wanted to take you now, hard and fast in the darkness, would that be the therapy you're looking for?"

She sucked in a breath. Perhaps he had gone too far. But the danger of the moment was like a sexual drug. They could do nothing but wait while their enemies searched for them. Adrenaline pounded in his veins. He'd been helpless to aid in their escape, and there was no way to contact Starforce now while they maintained a power-down silence. Any outgoing message might be enough to tip off the terrorists or the Raveners to their location. He needed to do something.

Her earlier request rang in his ears. Delivered in such a matter-of-fact manner, so calmly and coolly, he longed to heat her up, to bring her to the level of passion he'd glimpsed during their first embrace.

He'd give her some therapy that would make her bells

ring. The thought made him smile. Could she see his expression in the dim light?

"I think that's exactly the therapy I am looking for. Inarrii make poor liars, John Bennings. I mean it when I say I want you, but this is not the time." He could hear the frustration in her voice. "The Raveners have pinpointed you as a target. We nearly lost our lives—and two Inarrii warriors did die. Can you honestly say they are not looking for you specifically now? That they are not trying to find and kill you, a midlevel paper-pusher who should be of no importance to them?"

She was angry. And she was right. It wasn't the time. He pulled off his safety harness and stood. He would have paced the room but the dim light made it hard to see where it would be safe to burn off his frustration. Her use of his cover name bit at him. Two men had just died because of his cover. But the truth was that many more would die if the Treaty was not completed. He needed to go over the reports Davis had streamed him. Hell, he needed to get back to his assignment and find out what the fuck was going on. How in God's name had they tagged him? He gripped the edge of his seat and fought the urge to smash his fist against it.

"I'm sure the attack was simply convenient for Terran Purity. We were the last set of ships to leave the Osprey. They probably thought we weren't going to expect another attack at that point, and they would have gone after any Inarrii craft. Hitting a medtech ship is a terrorist tactic. They need to appear ruthless and unpredictable, but really they are using the same strategy that human terrorists have been exercising for centuries."

She stood and turned to face him. He could see the outlines of her body, but little else. "You seem to know a lot about this sort of warfare. And you knew about our surveillance base here. It isn't in use any longer, and while it isn't a secret between our governments, I doubt very many are aware of its existence. How *did* you know about it?"

He could feel the presence of her mind pressing lightly against his, questioning. She wasn't forcing her mind into his thoughts—from his intel reports that would have major moral repercussions for her people—but she was testing the water all the same. He pushed back, rejecting her inquiry. Somehow, he could almost taste her surprise at the action. Hell, *he* wasn't even sure what he had just done, but he felt a sagging relief when she pulled back. He didn't want to lie to her. She was doing her job, and doing it damn well, trying to protect him. But his duty came first.

"I'm curious. Maybe a little too curious, but that's all. I like to study battle strategy." He made a dismissive gesture, trying to put as much sincerity as he could bear into his tone. Lying was getting harder. He was putting what he could of the truth into his cover, even talking about the accident he'd had in the first year of the military, but it was starting to really rub at him. She didn't deserve it. "I'm sure that once they make a sweep of the area, the terrorists will pass us by and move on to an easier target. I am, after all, just a paper-pusher." The words tasted bitter on his tongue. When had keeping his cover ever been this hard?

"And if they don't leave?" Her voice told him she didn't believe they would, didn't believe him.

"I have every faith you will do everything you can to protect us." He thought fast. "But maybe we should move into the base itself. If they do discover us, it will give us some room to maneuver. They probably can't get deep enough into the tunnel to fire at us with those salvaged ships, so they'd have to come in here. If they're still looking for us."

Sarina didn't respond. If he were in her position, he wouldn't buy it either. There were cracks in his cover, and they were getting bigger. There were too many coincidences—the attacks on him, his knowledge of the base. And he didn't exactly fit the idea of a quiet lawyer either, or at least what she probably imagined as one. The way she'd latched on to the old human phrase "paper-pusher" said a lot.

She was smart, a fantastic strategist, and he couldn't wait to kiss her again. He wanted her, almost as much as he wanted one of the terrorists in his hands. He had questions for them. Terran Purity was definitely targeting him, and must have some way to track him. Having two objectives at once was a dangerous game. But if he could get Sarina to agree to move into the base, there was a chance he could achieve both goals.

He stepped closer to her, reached out to lightly touch the skin on her neck. When she didn't move to stop him, his mouth watered. The lines of her *L'inar* under the edge of her hair raised in thin ridges against the skin of his fingertips, and the muscles of her neck and shoulders were tight with tension.

HE WANTED HER AGAIN. It was the one thing that slipped past his mental shields, his sexual desire. The feeling stroked her senses, pulled at her until she longed for more than his light touch. She needed his fingers in her hair, his lips on hers. In the quiet of the darkened ship she wondered how much he could see of her. Could he see the yearning in her eyes? She could see him plainly—the slight strain in his chest muscles, the way his pulse throbbed in his neck, the rise in the material of his *pettan*.

Perhaps they would have time. Who knew how much Ravener technology had been transferred to the Terran purity ships? There was a chance the terrorists wouldn't be able to sense them inside the shelter of the rock tunnel. She and John could be alone for hours, with nothing to do but wait. The thought was intoxicating. She knew better than to hope for something her own people seemed unable to give her any longer. But she did wish he could begin again what they had started on board the Osprey. He almost seemed insulted that she viewed their sex as a therapy, but he obviously didn't understand the full importance of sexual completion to the Inarrii. He offered her something her own people couldn't—an unbiased view of their intimacy. He didn't see the flaws within her. He saw her as beautiful, desirable.

She leaned toward him, breathed in the clean, salty scent of his skin.

John's hand slid up from the back of her neck and into her hair. He caressed the *L'inar* on her scalp and she fought not to melt into his arms. He confused her. So sensual, so different than she'd imagined. Something about his story didn't really ring true, but what did she know of human culture? She could only understand her duty and what they experienced together, and so far that had alternated from dangerous to blessed good.

A small blinking light caught her attention. Their time alone would have to wait. The silent alarm was being triggered by an external sensor sweep. The terrorists were looking for them, and they were getting closer.

She pulled away from John. For a second he gripped her closer, resisting her attempt to pull away. She pointed to the display panel and the blinking alarm.

"Someone is scanning the craters for us," she whispered. "We're still in danger."

She stepped toward the communications unit. John moved with her, his hand resting on her shoulder as she tapped in an inquiry. She didn't need reassurance—she'd been a warrior all her adult life—but his touch made her sensitive to his closeness, to the seductive feeling of desire that seemed to follow him like a scent.

"It's the last ship that attacked us." There was no question now. She wouldn't argue it with John again, not just yet, but he was definitely the target. She had years of experience to back up her opinion. These people were searching for him, and they weren't giving up. It had been no random attack. He *was* the target.

"We can't call for help. An open channel would pinpoint us as clearly as if we shot a signal flare into space," John whispered back.

She nodded. "We are going to follow your idea. We will barricade ourselves in the base. If they do find the ship and follow us in, it will give us time while they try to get inside. We'll be more defensible and mobile. The human and Inarrii council will be expecting you in a few hours, and when you don't arrive they'll come looking for us."

"Well, let's make sure we're still here to be found."

"One way or another, we've only got hours before the moon's rotation puts us in the light and exposes the tail of the ship." Sarina tasted disappointment but she knew her job. She moved on to initiate lockdown on the shuttle. Once they'd gone out the doors no one would be able to enter and use the controls without a series of protocols that only those in her command chain were familiar with.

John caught her arm gently and pulled her close. "Hours can be long, Sarina. Long enough that you and I can find some time for each other." He lowered his head and pressed his lips to hers.

What began as a soft kiss threatened to devour her. For a long moment she let herself fall into the depths of his embrace. Somehow he knew what she'd been thinking, how desperate she was to feel something again with him. Ripples of sensation shuddered through her *L'inar*, rocking her with their intensity.

She prayed to the gods there would be time for everything John promised.

Chapter 6

"Okay, that's it. We're in full lockdown." Sarina palmed the control panel for the interior base hatch. "My DNA is coded into the security file. They'd have to blow the hatch to get in now."

"Perfect." John slipped a hand into his pocket and thumbed a microbug alive. Before they'd left the shuttle he'd had time to change into a basic shipsuit and grab the bag containing his personal effects. Much as he'd appreciated the way Sarina's eyes followed him while he was wearing the *pettan*, a full set of clothes on hand was a good thing, and so was the fact that no one had discovered his little trove of spy gadgetry. Tricks of the trade, some might call them, but in this situation, they might be the only way to maintain his cover and still perform his duty.

Sarina walked to the other side of the small room and placed a palm against what looked like a blank section of the wall. John blinked as the wall lit up under her touch, revealing a complex key and vid system. She concentrated on it, tapping various codes. John used her distraction to slide closer to the hatch and press the bug against the lock circuitry. It could be that the device would be ineffectual against Inarrii technology, but he was willing to take the chance. If he could get any additional information from the base for Starforce, it was a bonus, but more importantly he hoped the bug would give him some warning if the terrorists or Raveners made an attempt at opening the door—one that didn't involve just blowing it up.

"They're still looking for us, but they've moved to a different sector," Sarina spoke softly but didn't look up from the small display.

John mentally tagged the unit for the next bug—this must be a communication unit for her to be able to find out that information. Communications would be good. If there was any possibility of getting a message to Davis and therefore Starforce, this was it. He wouldn't risk contact while they were still being hunted, but if necessary he'd send a data dump at the last moment before they were captured or more probably killed—including every speck of information from the bugs on the Osprey and the ones here, and finally info on his own death.

Lights flickered on deeper into the hallway. Sarina was apparently reinitiating the power systems throughout the rooms and John was relieved to note the increase in ambient light. It made things a lot easier being able to see clearly. He glanced back at his Inarrii warrior bodyguard. It also helped to level the playing ground again between them. Sarina looked up and caught him staring at her. Damn, she was beautiful. Maybe not in a classic way, but it was perfect for him—her long nose and green eyes, shoulder-length hair and a body that could kick ass.

She seemed to sense his interest and stepped away from the comm pad. A few steps took her to the hallway. "I'm going to do a walk through. Stay here and I will return in a few minutes."

Before he could object she was through the doorway and headed down the hall. She was running from him, or maybe from his promise. John took a deep breath. The air didn't have the tang he expected from an abandoned base. The hydroponics oxygen system must still be active. Moving quickly, he set the second bug against the communications panel and pressed against it lightly. The unit seemed to melt into the electronics. John tapped his wrist comp, checking the link between the two bugs. The unit on the hatch was set to watchdog mode and seemed to be operating. The communications bug was silent. *Damn.* He swore under his breath. Hard to say if it was going to get him the access he needed or not.

John paced the length of the room. Now that Sarina had set the controls and lighting to a level where he could observe them, he found the glowing curved lettering on the walls and controls almost familiar. Their sinuous lines reminded him of Sarina's *L'inar.* There was nothing else he could do for the moment. They were being hunted, but it appeared as though they'd thrown their hunters off course for now. There was nothing to do but wait. If they came, he was ready for a siege situation—or as ready as he could be. He had his kit, good air and likely food, and a partner he could rely on.

It was a strange feeling—relying on anyone. It had been years since he could call anyone a partner, or even admit that he might want one. Davis didn't count; despite working with him for years, he rarely laid eyes on the man. Partners were people who could hurt you, just by being there. If something happened to your wingman, the emotional aspect alone might kill you. Make you unable to react in time... He forced his mind away from the past. The death of one friend was enough to make sure he'd never requested a new partner. Solo missions were more his style.

If the terrorists didn't come looking for them, it was only a matter of time before their people picked them up, and he could return to his mission, completing the Treaty and protecting the negotiators from within. If Sarina knew the truth about what he was, undercover protection, she might just want to join him. He thought of her impressive record. A real partner, one who wasn't the kind of rookie who got herself killed, could be a good thing.

But then, she could be more of a distraction than he could handle.

"To hell with this." Cover or not, he wasn't going to sit around thinking about something that wasn't likely to happen. He didn't have the clearance to tell her who he was, let alone ask her to help him. He wasn't even sure if he wanted to. John walked to the corridor. He was going to explore the Inarrii spy base. It was an opportunity not to be wasted. He could have a look at the Inarrii surveillance equipment, and the layout in case they were attacked. And if there was nothing else to learn he could find Sarina and take up what they'd left off, and this time he was going to take it slow. *Or maybe hard and fast and then slow.*

SARINA SLID the privacy door shut on the single sleep-room within the base and walked out into the corridor toward the hydroponics lab. She'd discovered the room minutes after leaving the control room. The last thing she'd needed was the sight of the large double-wide bed. Agent Gaerrii had taken the time to personalize the space some-what, programming the walls a dark red and installing a black carpet and air covers. Even the lighting had been dialed to the red tones of sunset at home. The overall effect reminded Sarina of how good it would be to lie on the beach on Inar again. And not alone.

If John cornered her in the bedroom, with his eyes full of desire and that soft ocean scent that seemed to emanate from his skin, Sarina would be doomed. She'd forget duty, forget the mission and reveal everything about herself and what she could no longer attain. She'd either jump on him or beg him for pleasure. Facing the traditional Inarrii bedroom, she realized that attempting sex, even as therapy, no longer seemed like a good idea. How could a human help her when an Inarrii Examiner had been unable to bring her to orgasm? And yet her soul clung to the desperate hope that he could somehow save her. She wasn't used to feeling helpless or indecisive. It rankled, gnawed at her. She ran her hands over the hilts of her *dash'tet* knives on her forearms as she walked into the corridor. There'd better be some action soon or she would lose all control.

Sarina strode through the corridor and into the large hydroponics production lab, halting abruptly when she realized she wasn't alone. Soft green light bounced up from the large, clear gel tanks, sending odd shadows dancing over John's body as he stood with his back to her. He'd spread his legs for balance as he leaned into the waist-high level two hydroponics tank and the thick layer of muscle along his back, legs and ass was clearly defined though his shipsuit. He reached into the tank and pulled out a handful of electro-fired bio gel. He couldn't hurt anything, touching the thick, wet slime, but she must have made some sound as she watched him because he turned to her. Light reflected off the transparent gel in his hands as he let it trickle through his fingers. His shipsuit was peeled back to his elbows to reveal powerful forearms.

His *m'ittar* reached for her in an inexperienced, yet graceful embrace of the mind. He was thinking of her, of how her body looked in the dark of the night in their shared rooms. She gasped. Linking with him sent ripples through her *L'inar*. His thoughts, mostly images, were lurid art painted across her mind.

He took a step toward her. Dazed by the power of his mental contact, she almost retreated, but he seemed to guess, or perhaps sense her hesitation through their shared thoughts. He moved quickly, stepping even closer until he could pull her into his arms. He wrapped his hand, still wet with the bio gel, around the base of her neck and lowered his mouth to hers. Her *L'inar* throbbed, stiffening into ridges under his slick fingers. The sensation spread, sending pulses of lust down her neck and spine. She moaned in his embrace. He took advantage of her weakness, and his tongue delved between her lips.

He tasted like the ocean, like the soft scent of his skin —salty sweet. *Dear gods, I am drowning.* And she wanted it. She wanted to slide beneath the waves with him. They were safe for now, hidden a mile under solid rock. The sensors would let her know before anyone found them. Why couldn't they take the time to explore each other?

He stroked her injured arm and reality slammed into her, breaking the waves of pleasure that were pulling her under.

"We can't do this, not now. They could be on us at any time." The excuse sounded like exactly that, an excuse, even to her ears.

"They're looking in a different section entirely. It could be hours before they return to this area, if ever. Our own people could be here first." He half thought, half murmured the words as he breathed against the tender flesh of her ear and neckline. The electro fired bio gel from his damp touch reacted to his breath and pulsed, enhancing the sensation. She groaned and the *L'inar* along her collarbone tightened, shooting a message of sexual desire that curved along the outer edge of her breast.

He was right. But still, she hesitated, and she hated herself for it. What Inarrii would say no when they had the time and their *L'inar* were tight with desire? But no matter what she felt in his arms now, she might not be able to find release. He stroked her arm and the nerve lines there didn't send their wicked pleasure along the outer abdominals lines on the way to her *sinaa* like they ought to. They couldn't, not any longer. If she couldn't find release now, perhaps she never would. Her belly tightened in a feeling that could only be fear. Did she really want to know if it could happen, one way or the other?

John pulled back but didn't let her go. He looked into her eyes. He knew. Somehow, he knew she was afraid. She could sense his understanding and that was as upsetting as the realization that she was afraid in the first place.

Warriors didn't have uncertainty. Uncertainty lead to inaction and that, led inevitably to death.

"We have time, Sarina," he murmured and she closed her eyes as he kissed her again. Warmth poured through their joined minds. He wanted her; she wanted him too. But what would be easy for any other Inarrii came slowly to her now. Instead of acting in response to the urges of her *L'inar*, she had to make a conscious choice. She breathed in the scent of his skin, touched his smooth neck. He stroked her back slowly through the hardy material of her fighting uniform, unconsciously caressing the rising nerve lines there. She opened her lips and let his tongue touch hers.

Finally she broke the embrace and looked into his eyes. She sent a pulse of desire and warmth along their *m'ittar*. "*Yes*."

He didn't speak. The soft hum of the hydroponics oxy system provided the only sound beyond their mingled breathing, and the submerged green lamps in the gel tanks gave off a light that was both surreal and sexual. Sarina pulled her auxiliary weapons harness from her shoulders. He moved to help her, easing the arm sheaths for her *dash'tet* from her forearms.

It was a slow seduction as he pulled her major weapons harness from her chest. He was disarming her, making her vulnerable, and her *L'inar* rippled with each layer he removed. It was as if he was peeling away the tough leather of a *mariin* fruit to reveal what lay beneath—the sweet flesh, and her soul. He kneeled to remove the second set of *dash'tet* knives from her calves. He tugged at her leg and she balanced on one foot as he pulled her boot off. There were no words, either spoken or thought, just his silent actions as he bared her skin and discarded everything that identified her as a warrior. Finally he began to remove the pressure-sensitive *tocuh* seals that held her uniform tightly shut against her body, tugging them free from his position on the floor.

Sarina pulled on his shipsuit collar. "Aren't you going to take this off too?" Her words caught in her throat, and she swallowed hard when his only response was to give her a lazy smile and to continue to open the seals. The top half of her uniform fell back, baring her breasts. After a little more tugging, the waist seal and leggings gave way as well and she was left standing naked before him. Every inch of her *L'inar*, even the disconnected lines on her arm, stood to rigid attention before his inspection.

Sarina cleared her throat. She'd been started at thousands of times during her recovery from the injury that damaged her *L'inar*, but never like this. Never with the heat of pure lust pouring over her through their connected thoughts. She shuddered, and her *L'inar* flattened and then pulsed into tight ridges once again. She felt her *sinaa* growing wet, throbbing with need. *Dear gods, this had better work.* If John could not bring her to orgasm at this level of response she was as good as dead, because she really would go insane.

He touched her then, laying the wide palms of his hands flat against her thighs. With a gentle push he nudged her back until her calves hit the slick surface of a low seat on one side of the tank behind her.

"I've been thinking of this since I met you." John's voice rasped against her ears, drew a gasp of breath from her lips. The level of his desire washing over her through their *m'ittar* contact was overwhelming. "I didn't take my time before. Now I need to touch you. Lay back."

Sarina sat on the couch. It was a simple padded bench, but right now she couldn't have cared if it was a rough wooden plank. Heat pooled in her *sinaa* as she imagined his lips there, his tongue invading her depths. But as she lay back John lifted one of her legs, kissing the curving arch of her foot. Surprise flickered though her and sent her nerve lines dancing along the inner lines of her thighs. Slowly he licked the sensitive flesh of her sole, teased his tongue into the area between her toes.

His action confused her, caused her heart to race. When she would have pulled back he moved closer to the bench and bent her leg at the knee until her hips opened. He used one hand to trace the extremely sensitive *L'inar* lines above her knee and up her thigh until he worked closer to her *sinaa*. She felt exposed; her heart pounded harder with excitement. With each caress he nibbled the edge of her foot. Sensation warred within her—the strangeness of his attention toward her foot knocked against the intense pleasure of the rough edge of his nail dragging against her fully aroused nerve lines.

Just as she relaxed, he sucked the first of her toes into his hot wet mouth.

"What are you doing?" She sent the question through their linked mind and felt him respond. She could sense his pleasure at being able to touch her in any way he chose. Lust flickered through him at the sense of control and she gasped. She was experiencing his pleasure, could literally feel the anticipation and throbbing tightness of his cock. She jerked back but he held tight and gave her heel a little nip and her inner thigh a light slap.

Pleasure, with the slightest hint of pain, radiated through her from her thigh. This time *he* gasped.

"I can feel you…" His metal voice was a whisper but much clearer than she expected.

"This isn't normal—" she began, but he gave her other thigh a quick slap as well and her thoughts were scattered as they both rocked with the sensation.

"I like feeling you. In fact, I intend to feel everything." His thoughts were stronger now, his excitement giving them a power she would never have expected from an untrained *m'ittar*.

Sarina worked to recover from her shock, but he was quicker, and she almost didn't see him reach back to the tank and grab a handful of the bio gel. Her eyes widened as he grinned at her. Before she could ask what he was doing, he began to spread the tingling slime over her feet and up the length of her calves. The warm gel carried a small electric charge to encourage the growth of oxygen-producing bacteria, but tank two was a clean, nonliving area. She tried to pull away, but as he soothed the charged gel against her skin she relaxed. It felt...like her *L'inar* reached her very toes.

"You know," she said, sighing in pleasure through their link, *"this much electro gel costs more than my annual salary."*

He laughed and the sound bounced against her with a burst of warmth. She realized then that their link was strong enough for him to hear her. That wasn't always possible between human and Inarrii. She nearly joined him in laughter, but he nudged her and she willingly rolled over. He began to rub the gel into the delicate skin behind her knees. She moaned, already imagining what the tingling warm goo would feel like being massaged into her *L'inar*. His hands on her were a contrast of cool skin and heated gel. More, she could almost feel the silken texture of her skin through his thoughts.

"You like this. I like this. Who the hell cares what anything costs." She heard his jumbled message and relaxed further, until he slathered the first handful of gel up the backs of her thighs and across her ass. Then she heard nothing, felt nothing except the throbbing of her *L'inar* as they reacted to the electric charge of the gel, the caress of his fingers. Each segment that he brushed with gel sent sensation directly to her *sinaa* in a shuddering wave of ecstasy.

"John," she groaned aloud. She writhed beneath his hands as they painted her hips and sides with gel. She pulled her weight up onto her knees and pressed back against him, half sobbing with need and disappointment when she realized he was still clothed. The rough material of his shipsuit dragged against her nerve lines and she shuddered.

He reached under her and fingered the hard, thin ridges of her *L'inar* patterns around the wet pool of her *sinaa*, finally dipping inside. When she cried out in pleasure, his moan matched hers. She could feel the tightness of his cock through his shipsuit and realized suddenly that he was using his clothing as a last measure to control his own reaction.

"I want you inside me." She managed to pass the message through their thoughts.

The sweet sound of his shipsuit being opened rewarded her efforts.

His body pressed against hers, the cool, clean skin of his belly and hips sticking to the layer of charged bio gel on her ass. The hard outline of his cock pressed against her. He held her tightly against his chest for just a moment, his breath a ragged sound in her ear. But he wasn't finished, wasn't ready to take her. She nearly begged for mercy when he pulled away. Where was her warrior determination now? She could only whimper when he fought his own desire and continued to spread the charged gel up her back, stroking her nerve lines with each pass of his hand.

Wild, uncontrolled ripples of sensation undulated through her *L'inar*. He flipped her over, his strength far beyond hers at this moment. She could only ride the waves of pleasure as he continued to coat her in the clear gel. He was half covered in it himself and her mind buzzed with the overlapping of his experience with hers. There were no words for it. He caressed her breasts with wet fingers, tracing the lines of her stiffened *L'inar*. Muted recognition whispered though her; his actions followed the wet trail that lips and tongue would have traced if he were an Inarrii pledging his desire to permanently mate.

She bucked under him, rubbing her soaking *sinaa* against his cock. Now she did beg, with her body and voice. "Please, John."

Sarina kissed his chest in desperation, feeling the crisp hairs with her lips, and their mind contact tightened. She was aware of his skin where her lips touched it, and the pleasure he felt at her abandon. It had been too long since her last orgasm, and she shuddered with need. At this moment she would have agreed to do anything for him, and through their link he knew it.

But he held back, dripped more gel over her breasts and nipples, painting every inch of her skin. Everything was wet, their bodies gliding together with only the tingling gel between them.

John pulled back and she moaned in dismay. But he took a seat on the bench beside her and caught her up by her upper arms. He pulled her up on top of him. She cried out as the gel on his hands coated the scars on her upper arm and connected her severed *L'inar* to the whole nerves on her upper shoulder, just as he positioned her over his cock. Her body thrilled, and she trembled in reaction as nerves met. He chose that instant to lower her *sinaa* onto him, impaling her and making her whole all at once.

She rocked on his cock, so much thicker than any Inarrii, and rode the waves of her first orgasm in months. Wave after wave crested over her. She pulled nearly off of him only to plunge down again and again. Her final peak tore a scream from her lips.

John cried out her name as he thrust under her. He was coming, his orgasm hot inside her before hers had even begun to subside. The pleasure was intense; she could feel the pressure build and explode within him. Her *sinaa* clenched tight around him as she shuddered in a second orgasm. The power of the combined ecstasy bouncing between them wrung a scream from her throat and she rocked again with him until they lay spent in each other's arms.

She shivered against him. Finally, she was once again more than a warrior at the end of her days. She felt like a person again, wonderfully female and alive.

Chapter 7

"**D**amn," John managed after long moments of silence. Sarina shivered at his exclamation. "That was so good, but so fast. I wanted to go slow…" He panted the words, but they failed to express what he felt. There was no way to explain what he'd experienced with her, the way that for long moments pressed against her he felt a part of something greater, or how he wanted it to go on, and never stop.

"I know, but I couldn't wait. I needed you."

Her thoughts sounded as clear to him as if she had spoken aloud. Mind contact was so much more than he had imagined. When she came he couldn't hold back; his orgasm had rushed to meet hers as he felt each throbbing pulse of her pleasure. It had been fast but was also easily the most erotic experience of his life, feeling her pulse all around him and within him as she tipped over the edge and gave herself up completely to the sensation. She pulled him with her, the lines of her *L'inar* burning along his skin as they tightened on hers.

But if she thought he was finished, she was wrong.

He let go of her arms and she sagged against his chest, her eyes closed. Carefully he began to trace the nerve lines, now nearly flat, around her hip bones. She murmured something he couldn't understand and then repeated it again, louder as he stroked the few thin lines that edged the curves of her ass.

"*Ya'sai lenali.*"

He rolled his hips, testing his half-hard cock within her. He could still feel her pleasure, the echo of each thing she was experiencing, nearly as strongly as his own sensual reaction to their bodies touching. *Dear God, if this is what sex is always like between the Inarrii, no wonder it's so important to them.* Carefully he levered himself down flat on the long, low bench and pulled her along with him until her full weight centered on him. She was completely relaxed, her muscles lax to his touch.

"What does that mean? *Ya'sai lenali?*"

"It means…more, please."

His cock hardened. There were a hundred ways he wanted to give her more. The hard warrior woman had dissolved in his arms until she was pure sex. Both versions of Sarina had more appeal than any of the women he'd slept with in the last year.

"*You have had sex with many women.*"

John gripped her a little closer. She was catching small pieces of his thoughts. But things could go two ways. "*You have spent too much time alone.*"

"*It's hard to find a partner at times, even among bunkmates on a mission.*" She replied through their link but avoided his underlying question as easily as he had slipped past hers.

The use of her word, partner, tugged at him, reminded him of his earlier thoughts on why he worked alone. "*Bunkmates are better than partners. Less of a distraction.*"

She looked at him, her bright green eyes still faintly clouded with pleasure. "*Caring for a partner makes you fight harder to protect them.*"

The thought was too deep for him to handle right now. He wanted to pleasure her, to bring her a level of ecstasy that would make them both forget their past. John scraped a finger over the *L'inar* along Sarina's outer thigh and gathered a layer of bio gel from her skin. The gel tingled, still maintaining its mild charge. Each touch resonated within him as he felt her react in pleasure. His own thigh quivered, and answering throbs of pleasure wound within his cock, just as they pulsed within Sarina. *M'ittar* ecstasy. He imagined how good it would feel to go down on her, for both of them. Slowly he began to rock his hips, pulling his cock out of her slightly and rocking it back inside. She moaned and lifted her hips, put her weight on her knees and giving him more room. She pressed her mouth against his neck, licking the soft skin above his collarbone.

John slid his wet finger down the curve of Sarina's ass and pressed it against her tight opening. She gasped, her body shuddering as he penetrated her slightly. John jerked as the sensation echoed through their mind contact. He thrust his cock harder into her and used his other hand to stroke the rippling nerve lines along her back. Pleasure streaked across his body.

"I didn't think I could feel this again." Her thoughts passed to him on a crest of sensation.

"Why not?" He brushed the thought back to her, softly, like a silent whisper.

"My L'inar, they are broken. I am broken…"

"You seem fine to me." John replied lightly but his heart clenched. She believed herself to be damaged. The urge to prove to her that she was perfect for him surged, but he kept his pace steady. Her emotions were erratic, filtering through to him through her pleasure. What would she feel from him? She might take concern for pity, and that would be the last thing she needed. Instead he poured desire through their link and focused on her body.

He was fucking her, taking her with cock and fingers and possessing her, and at the same time he was experiencing what she felt as she submitted and was overcome by sensation. It was almost too much, but her need washed over him and he took more, slowly fucking her ass and her pussy, driving her with sensation and accepting it himself until she whimpered and covered his neck and chest in a pattern of kisses only she could understand.

THIS WAS EXACTLY what she had needed. Total, utter release. She pulsed around him, the muscles of her pussy milking come from him as they rocked together in orgasm. He was perfect, accepting their link like he was born to it and using it to cascade his experience into her mind until their combination of pleasure spiked within her.

Finally Sarina lay down against John's heaving chest. Beyond the soft hum of machinery and their quick breaths, she heard the strong muscle of his human heart slow to a more regular rhythm beneath her. Relief poured through her until she trembled with the power of it. She would not lose her mind, not have to see her career crumble, not have to end her life before she became a burden to her clan.

"Shh." John made a soft noise and cuddled her closer.

Even his gentle caress against the flattened nerve lines on her back was a source of joy. She could relax, knowing he could help her find release again when she needed it. He'd be happy to. She lifted her head from his chest to look at his face and then grimaced at the way her cheek stuck to him. The bio gel had finally cooled and lost its charge.

"Come on, let's go get cleaned up." She pulled herself away from him, despite the fact that part of her would prefer to lay there against him, possibly for days. Being so close to someone again, knowing they could find joy in each other's arms, it was something she hadn't known was so important until it was taken from her. But there wasn't time to think about that now.

They were still at risk in the tiny base. She couldn't find it in herself to regret the time they'd taken together; it relieved the stress and made them both more alert and ready. The proximity alarm hadn't triggered during their idyll together, but it was only a matter of time before their enemy searched the area more thoroughly. John was a target of the Ravener and Terran Purity alliance. He was no ordinary paper-pushing lawyer. Something about him was more. He was bringing the danger to them. And yet, he might be the only one whose *m'ittar* meshed with hers to the point where she forgot herself and experienced only their combined sensations. He made her whole again.

She tightened her jaw muscles. Determination sent strength flooding through her system. She *was* whole again, and she'd be damned if she would fail at her mission. Her clan might have accepted her as a lost cause, but she would prove them wrong.

John groaned as she rolled off of him, but he levered himself up on the bench and rubbed a hand over his face. "God, woman. You blow my mind with wicked sex and then you want to hop right up and get moving again?"

He complained, but she sensed the humor and acceptance in his words. Their link hadn't faded completely; it still remained in the background despite the fact that they were no longer touching. A tiny finger of satisfaction wrapped around her. She'd had an affect on him. They'd joined minds in a rare mirror link and his walls hadn't completely returned afterward. She smiled at him and he grinned back. She picked up her uniform and weapons harness and he snagged his shipsuit and bag, along with both their boots.

Satisfaction edged into worry and she turned away, headed for the cleanser unit attached to the sleeproom. They'd formed an attachment, but it wasn't one that could last. They were from different worlds, literally and figuratively. What if he was the only one who could join with her? No Inarrii seemed willing to try, and she had no idea how many humans had enough *m'ittar* to form a mirror link. It was extremely rare, even among Inarrii. Desperation beat an uncomfortable rhythm in the pit of her belly.

What if she couldn't reach completion without it? What if John was her only mirror?

She hurried to the ultrasonic cleanser, dumping her things on the floor nearby. John followed only a few steps behind. Her thoughts raced back and forth. How had they achieved the sensory mirror? Was it something unique to John, or the combination of their two minds? Or was it the situation, the danger and their intense shared desire? She thought back to the various medtechs that had discussed her case. No one had mentioned anything like this to her as a possible treatment. She paused before she opened the cleanser unit. Medtech Yassin had said something about electro gel just before they had discussed John's status on the medtech shuttle. For the first time since her injury, she wished she'd spent more time with the medical staff. Could the gel have been the answer?

"What's wrong?" John touched her shoulder. His concern echoed over their link. She was sensing his emotions, vague feelings rather than specific directed thoughts and images. The rest of his mind was shut again, but that was for the best—she had no desire to share her personal worries, or her suspicions.

Sarina opened the cleanser. "Nothing. But I'll feel better being dressed and prepared, just in case someone comes looking for us."

John's lips tilted down slightly at the corners.

She turned away and stepped into the cleanser. She reached to shut the door behind her, but he blocked the door with his body as he climbed into the unit with her, pressing her nearly to the back wall. He pulled the door shut behind him.

"Are you sorry we had sex?" His blunt question took her off guard. It was a question no Inarrii would ask, because who would regret finding release in the arms of the willing?

"No. Of course not." She emphasized her surprise and rejection at the idea through their link. His gray eyes seemed cooler now. She looked away. How could she admit that she was worried that it might not happen again? Or that it would, but only with him? More frightening than anything else, a final question whispered inside her—what if she could experience release with someone else, but she only ever wanted him?

Sarina initiated the cleanse cycle. The hum of ultrasonic waves vibrated from the top of her scalp down through to the bones in her heels and then worked its way back up again. The sound of John's quick intake of breath caught her attention.

"Is this your first time in a sonic unit?" She sent the thought to him.

"Yes. I've only been on board an Inarrii ship once, and not for a long stay." John relaxed under the pulse, rolled his shoulders and stretched. His muscular frame looked exotic and sexy; his smooth skin was so different from hers, and the tiny hairs on his arms and chest and legs moved slightly with the ultrasonic waves as the gel was removed from his skin. He raised his arms and rested his palms against the sides of the unit, taking up far too much space. She had no choice but to lean into him. Immediately their link strengthened. She nearly moaned as she received his impression of the warm rhythm of the cleanser, especially as it passed over his balls and cock.

She did gasp as an image from his mind slipped through the link—her on her knees in the cleanser sucking his cock as she would an Inarrii *saiin*, the sonic waves set to a rhythm that matched the pace of her mouth dragging along his skin. He would like to possess her in this way, holding her head and pumping into her mouth as she did her best to suck his seed into her throat until she swallowed. Her *sinaa* pulsed, immediately wet in reaction to a scene that nearly reflected the final part of an Inarrii mating ceremony.

JOHN SNAPPED alert as Sarina pushed past him and out of the cleanser. She broke their mental link as she shut the door between them, leaving him in the cleanser while she left the room entirely. He checked his wrist comp but the sensors on the hatch to the base remained on watchdog mode; no attempt had been made to breach the entrance.

"Sarina?" He called to her but she didn't answer. He shut the cleanser down and pushed open the door. Worry nibbled at him, and a quick rush of adrenaline slammed through his veins. He checked the other bug, but the communications panel remained silent. There was no way of knowing if this was because nothing was being picked up, or if the microbug simply couldn't access this level of Inarrii technology.

Whatever was wrong, she'd taken her clothes and her weapons, and even her boots. Years of training had him yanking his microknives from the hidden pocket in his bag before hauling his shipsuit on up to his waist. The knives weren't as good as a hand laser, but there was no way to get one through the various levels of security on the Osprey. The only one he had access to while undercover was still strapped to the outside of the Osprey's hull.

He strained his ears but couldn't hear any sign of alarm. He sat on the edge of a low couch and pulled on his boots. Whatever had pushed Sarina into action, it didn't seem to be an immediate attack. John took a moment to slide a microknife into the top of each boot and the cuffs of his shipsuit as he pulled it the rest of the way on. The thin blades were nearly unbreakable, and were sharp enough to slice perma plas. They made hand-to-hand combat a deadly affair.

John took a closer look at the bedroom. The dominating colors, red and black, probably represented the Inarrii home world. He considered just how little he knew of the Inarrii and of Sarina in particular. He had the information from the intel reports, and she'd mentioned a few details about clan structure, but other than the fact that she'd been injured, he knew very little about her personally. He wanted to know more. She believed she was broken in some way he couldn't understand. It seemed more complicated than the fact that her *L'inar* had been severed. He wanted to understand her. More than how she responded during sex, although he was far from finished exploring that topic.

He'd just been thinking of round three in the cleanser when she broke everything off and nearly ran from the room. He shut his eyes and shook his head at his own stupidity. He'd been thinking of taking her mouth while she was on her knees in front of him. He knew damn well she could feel what he did. Did she sense what he wanted from her? Did she find his fantasy degrading? Starforce had very strict rules on relations between ranks, and any hint of sexual dominance was strictly forbidden.

Then it struck him and he groaned aloud. Intel had reported on the marriage ceremonies of the Starforce Marine Susan Branscombe to the now Inarrii/human Ambassador, Asler Kiis. Most of it had been blocked due to the personal nature of the ceremony, but enough was stated that he should know oral sex had some serious implications. He'd either scared her off or offended her.

A quick vibration against his wrist from his comp brought John back from his thoughts. He tapped the small unit and was rewarded with a connection to the Inarrii communications system. His little bug had come through. He ran a hand over his jaw. Between flight time and the time spent on the base, he'd been out of contact with Davis for nearly four hours. Time enough for his absence to be reported. They wouldn't be able to send a search party immediately, not without blowing his cover, but they would have scanned his reported flight path by now and alerted the Inarrii to the wreckage of the *sho'tet* blade ships that had been sent with them as escort. Rescue would soon be on the way.

The risk of sending a message should be minimal. He

needed more information before he made his next move. And finding out just how badly he might have pissed off his Inarrii bodyguard might also be a good idea. He initiated the secure channel.

"Davis, this is Bennings. Can you read?" John sent the security code along with his query. If Davis could hear him, they were good to go.

"John! I was beginning to think you were dead. Where the hell are you?"

"On the abandoned Inarrii surveillance base on the moon. We were attacked by more of the Terran Purity group. They took out our two escorts. And I can confirm they have more fire power than they ought to."

"Well, I'm glad you're still up and running. There haven't been any other reported attacks, only you. They have you pinned somehow."

John shook his head. Davis loved to state the obvious. "No shit. We were forced into hiding here."

"We? I take it that curvy bodyguard's still with you."

John stood. "Yeah, she's here. But I need more intel. How the hell has Terran Purity managed to pin us? What have they got for scanning tech? You'd better get a message to the CIC to get us out of here soon." He hesitated and rubbed a hand against his tense shoulder. "And I need access to the Starforce database on Inarrii personal conduct."

"You've got whatever we have on the terrorist capabilities as we know them. No info on the scanning ability. And what the hell do you need alien etiquette lessons for? Just screw her like you usually do and get the hell out of there."

"Fuck off, Davis. Just send me the data." He stared at this wrist comp and was relieved to see the data stream flowing through the connection.

"Wow, you did it already, didn't you? You had the alien bitch on her knees. Are they really ridged inside and out?" Davis laughed, the unpleasant sound coming in all too clearly through the wrist unit. "Screw her all you like. Just don't let her *think* at you."

"We're done here. Get the message to the CIC." John clicked off the channel. His temples pounded. They *were* done, for good. He'd worked for years with Davis and had always considered him an okay guy, even a little funny. But the asshole had a real problem with the Inarrii, one that had now gone way over the line. There was something wrong with him. If he'd been standing in the room right at this moment, John would have put his fist through the mission tech's face.

And deep in his gut, John knew that could only mean one thing…

SARINA SLAPPED the final seal shut on the last of her exterior weapons harness. "*Ken stasht,*" she swore aloud. Things were getting too complicated. She knew damn well John hadn't been proposing a mating—the human probably had no idea what kind of image his fantasy presented to her. He just wanted to continue their sexual play. So did she, for that matter.

What had her worried was that she would be considering more sex when they were still in danger. They were concealed from the enemy on a barely defendable abandoned base. Even if it was accepted practice to get close to the person you were supposed to protect, there was a time and place for everything. She'd ignore the fact that she couldn't find it in herself to say no the first time. She'd needed the stress relief too badly. This time she would stay in control and do her duty to protect him.

Perhaps she had gone too long without release. Maybe her mind was already damaged if all she could think about was the fact that not only did the sex sound nearly irresistible, but the idea of mating was starting to sound damn good too. Not that John had meant to offer anything more.

She shook her head at her own folly. She was a warrior. Even if he had offered...what could she have in common outside of the bedroom with a man who worked with facts and figures all day? A small voice spoke within her mind, reminding her of his claim to study a human fighting art, and the way he considered strategy when he revealed his knowledge of the Inarrii surveillance base. Perhaps they weren't that different.

Alarms chimed from the control panel to her right. "*Ken stasht*," she whispered. Somehow she'd ignored the first signal indicating the terrorists were back and were scanning the area—either she'd not heard it or the alarm simply hadn't triggered. Now they were coming in fast. She checked the visual. A shuttle had already wedged itself against the medtech ship, blocking their only escape. In minutes they would be at the entrance.

She slapped her hands against the controls and pulled up the security codes. It took a long minute, too long, to try and pull up a secondary shield over the main hatch. When the effort proved useless, she cursed. The base was never meant to defend against attacks; it was only a short-term surveillance position. It didn't have the defense protocol that might have at least given them more time.

Sarina unholstered her hand laser. The entrance was between her and John, and the terrorists would be through it in a matter of moments. She'd headed for the control room after leaving John. A little space between them seemed like a good thing at the time, but now she was here and he was probably back in the bedroom, alone and unarmed. Her *L'inar* rippled as she realized she didn't even know for sure where he was, and she had no way to contact him.

She could hear them now, cutting through the hatch that she'd sealed to her DNA code. In less than a minute she would see the laser beam cutting through the final layer of the hatch. No time to plan anything. Sarina dove from the control room and past the entrance, rolling as she hit the floor, and twisted to face the approaching attack.

Two hands grabbed her shoulders and she grunted in surprise. John's *m'ittar* touched hers and she allowed him to pull her through the door into the main corridor. She kept her laser focused on the hatch, ready for the first shot when the terrorists cut through. A line of black formed on the metal as the first laser punched through. Licks of flame darted up from the line as lasers burned hot enough to melt the metal.

"Shit." John swore as the automated fire suppression system kicked in, coating the hatchway in a layer of directed foam. Smoke poured into the air. Visibility dropped and he tugged on Sarina's arm. *"We need to get out of here."* His mental voice was insistent, but calm.

"Back to the hydroponics lab." She sent him the direction and was relieved when he let her go and headed deeper into the base.

She followed, retreating backward while she covered their movement. They had made it nearly halfway through the corridor when she heard the hard clang of cut metal hitting the floor. They weren't coming in silent—they either didn't expect any resistance or just didn't care if they took some losses and were counting on the superiority of numbers. Either way, she was going to make sure they regretted it.

Chapter 8

"Duck under the oxygen pump. They won't fire in here—it could blow the entire base if they hit the generator with laser fire." Sarina pointed out an empty spot, just big enough for John to fit under.

He shot her a look that matched the feeling of incredulity in his *m'ittar*. *"I'm not getting under there."*

Sarina holstered her hand laser. She couldn't risk a shot any more than the terrorists would inside the hydroponics lab. There were too many volatile elements. *"We don't have time to argue about this. They are here for you, and I intend to see they don't manage to kill you."*

John pressed his lips into a look of grim determination. Somehow he'd armed himself. She grimaced. The man was definitely not a lawyer. He must have brought the set of small blades with him—they were nothing like her *dash'tet*. A flare of anger arced through her at his continued deception, but she tamped it down. Knives in each of his hands glinted in the warm green light of the lab. She shook her head at him, but it was his choice. She'd simply make sure they didn't reach him. No matter what he really was, it was still her job to protect him.

Sounds of running feet reached her seconds before the first attacker barreled through the doorway and into the lab. She dropped low and snapped out one leg, bringing him down for a moment while the second attacker charged into the room as well. Sarina thrust upward, extending her body and her arms as she drew her first *dash'tet*. The large knife snagged on the rough material of her opponent's shipsuit, but not before it did its damage—a large slice up the man's mismatched chest armor.

Both attackers appeared human, and they wore ragged uniforms that had seen better days. Sarina's mind automatically categorized them as members of the terrorist group Terran Purity. She pulled back a step, giving herself room to maneuver, but kept her body between them and John's location.

The man on the floor sprang back to his feet. His eyes rolled in their sockets and he panted hard. Anger and hunger were fueled by insanity, his emotions roaring out at her *m'ittar* as he lunged for her. Sarina twisted to one side, evading his strike. He held a laser rifle in both hands and was using the long barrel as a thrusting weapon. Sarina moved faster. He could forget, given his state of mind, that they were beside the main oxygen tank and fire at her, blowing the entire base. She had to take him down first. Her second opponent was still in shock and gripping the edges of his plated chest armor, probably unsure if her strike had been deep enough to be fatal.

The crazy man began to shriek at her, words she couldn't understand and wouldn't matter in a few moments. Sarina released the strap on her second *dash'tet*. With a long bade in both hands, she slashed at him. He blocked the first blow with the laser rifle but she'd expected that. Instead of pulling back for a second strike she moved in closer, until she was only inches away from his face, and ran the edge of her blade along the barrel of his weapon. The *dash'tet* found its mark and the man lost his grip on the laser as she sheared his fingers from his hand. Her second blade found its way into his gut and lodged deep under his rib bones.

He crumpled in front of her.

A noise from the side caught her attention. She turned and extended her *dash'tet* in a single, smooth motion, leaving behind her other knife, which was wedged in the first opponent. The sharp edge sliced a second gouge over the terrorist's armor, this time a fatal cut. He fell back and down against the edge of the doorway without a single word. Blood sprayed over her, tinted black in the green light of the hydro tanks.

Two humans down, definitely dead or dying, but she had no time to do more than grasp the victory. A blow, shudderingly hard, hit her from the back, the strength of it nearly bringing her to her knees. She tried to twist away but her attacker was too fast. She reeled from a second strike, this time to the side of her head, and lost her grip on her second long knife. She couldn't get a good visual—he moved too fast for a human and hit too hard. She caught a burst of movement out of the corner of her eye. She cried out in frustration as she realized John had entered the fight. He slashed at the terrorist and missed. The man twisted like an earth snake and hit John hard from the side. The bastard had a knife of his own; John's shout of pain told Sarina he'd been cut.

Sarina hit the ground and rolled, catching the attacker's legs and entangling him. John reacted as smoothly as if they had trained together for years, dodging the struggling attacker to slide in and stab him in the side. The man snarled, swearing in a language Sarina recognized.

"Gathan shit!" She kicked at him from the ground, using the strength of her legs to keep the alien from recovering his balance. Again John went in for a strike and connected, his microknives flashing as he drew the creature's thick blue blood, but he was thrown back after a single hit.

Sarina twisted to the side and gained her feet. She pulled both *dash'tet* from her leg holsters. John charged at the same time that she leaped. They hit the Gathan from the back and side, and he went down with a sickening crunch. Sarina listened but couldn't hear anything but her pounding heart and John's panting breaths. Finally she caught a wheezing sound from the alien. He lived, barely. She stood and staggered to the doorway, sliding her long knife home and drawing her laser. She checked the corridor. Empty. She turned back to the hydroponics lab. John clutched at his shoulder, applying pressure to the slash he'd received that the hands of the Gathan. Red blood and blue spattered the floor in slick patterns, but the three attackers lay motionless.

John nudged the Gathan with his foot then bent to pull a band of glowing metal from its neck. Immediately the wounded man's form wavered and changed, revealing his true elongated shape and blue skin. "Not human."

"No, it's a Gathan. We rejected them from Confederation membership. They joined the Raveners after that, but some think that was their plan all along. That they only applied for membership to take a good look at our defenses. They are the ones providing the human terrorists with the weapons and technology."

John nodded and pocketed the Gathani device. He winced.

Sarina sucked in a breath as she realized he was still bleeding. "How badly are you hurt?" She holstered her laser and *dash'tet* and walked to him. Carefully she ran her hands over his shipsuit, checking for further slashes.

"Bad enough, but he really only got the shoulder. It's a clean cut. No tendon damage, I don't think." He pointed his chin toward the motionless Gathan. "Is he going to make it?"

She glanced down at the wounded man. "Does he have to?"

"Bandage him and tie him up. I have a few questions I'd like to ask him." John's deep tone hummed with anger and power. Not exactly the voice of a lawyer.

"I bet you do."

JOHN SLUMPED into the control chair. His shoulder hurt like a bastard, and helping to drag the fucking blue guy through the corridor hadn't helped. The alien was impossibly heavy, made from something far denser than human tissue. He watched as Sarina shoved the Gathan into the spare seat. She tapped the seal on a wall compartment, sliding out a drawer full of equipment. John grinned. Alien toys.

She slapped a set of force-bindings against the Gathan's legs and arms. The bindings emitted a low hum and glowed orange as they constricted against the alien's skin. John shook his head. The Gathani technology that transformed him from a blue giant to a normal-looking human was amazing. The other two attackers had been human—members of Terran Purity and probably completely unaware that they worked beside an alien from outer space, the same sort of creature they claimed to be protecting the Earth from.

"He's secure. Now it's your turn." Sarina pulled a small case from the same drawer and walked over to him. Her fingers trembled as she pulled open his shipsuit to look at the damage done to his shoulder.

"It's not that bad, Sarina."

Tiny tremors flickered along the *L'inar* on her neck. He concentrated on the lines as they tensed into thin ridges and flattened again. He loved the swirl of reddish brown color, like a henna tattoo, a decorative art he might never tire looking at. He sucked air as she examined the slash in his skin and a flare of pain followed her touch.

"You should have stayed out of the fight. It's my job to protect you."

"Is that what's really bothering you?"

She ran a cleanser pad over his skin and he winced. She froze. She was upset, beyond the stress that would be normal for the aftermath of a near-death situation, especially for an experienced warrior like her. He thought of her recent injury. There was no medlab here and she was forced to treat his wounds because he couldn't reach them, making due with the same kind of basics he could have found on any human outpost.

"How badly were you injured, Sarina?" He filled his thoughts with gentle reassurance. If he was right, seeing his injury brought back thoughts of her own.

"Laser burns to one arm. My arm was nearly cut off…my L'inar were severed."

"Did it take long to heal?"

She was moving again, disinfecting the slice and applying a pressure pad. *"My L'inar were burned away from my central column. They will never heal."*

A wave of sorrow passed through her *m'ittar*. John fought not to react too quickly through the mental link. Something about the way she spoke of her injury, the impression he received through her emotions, told him she was talking for the first time about how her injury had really affected her. It amazed him that she would reveal something so personal to him. It touched him in a way nothing ever had.

"Without L'inar, I am…incomplete. I am not whole."

A strange ache formed in John's chest as he listened to the words that whispered hesitantly in his mind and the emotions that flavored them, bitter and salty, like angry tears. *"I don't understand."*

"Without L'inar, there is no completion. Inarrii must experience complete sexual release regularly or they lose their mind. It is only a matter of time before I do the same."

John stared at her in disbelief. Her green eyes reflected utter sincerity. She believed that she was going to go crazy, that she was a lost cause. *"Forgive me, but I believe we've just proven that theory wrong."*

"Perhaps."

John winced as Sarina pulled the bandage tighter on his shoulder, keeping the pressure on to make sure it would stop bleeding. She was far from convinced, but their experience together left no doubt in his mind. He could still feel the way she shuddered in ecstasy. She'd flown with him, and he could think of a hundred different ways to make it happen again. The urge to protect her, to heal her and make her believe in herself grew from a small glow within him to a bright point of focused desire.

But first his duty required him to focus on his primary mission. He glanced over to their hostage, now tied to the spare seat in the control room. The blue-skinned alien sagged against his bindings. Dragging the Gathan up here had hurt more than the original slice to his shoulder. But the control room offered options for interrogating the pirate. John *would* have the answers he needed, one way or another.

"I think he'll be out for a bit. You hit him pretty hard." Sarina spoke aloud before turning away.

"All that karate practice finally paying off." John shrugged the sleeve of his shipsuit over the bandages on his shoulder. The thick material was even stiffer than usual, now that it had been coated in blood.

She turned back to him. He could almost taste her annoyance in the air between them, a flavor he could do without if he wanted to maintain his cover. A small voice inside him reminded him that he *didn't* actually want to maintain it. He wanted to get it over with and tell her. At least then they could work with the same level of intel. Right now she was protecting him without knowing the real reasons behind the attacks, and in truth he couldn't see the purpose behind it. If he had clearance, he'd give her full access in a heartbeat.

"Do you really want to keep going with that story?"

"Sarina," John reached for her. "I'm sorry."

A LOW MOAN caught Sarina's attention. She broke her eye contact with John and glanced over at their captive. With a sudden jerk, the Gathan prisoner snapped alert. He emitted a low snarl and then pressed his thin lips tightly together as he eyed his captors. Sarina glanced from him to John and caught the relief within his *m'ittar* before he snapped the connection shut. Her mind groped for his, but for a man with no training in mental arts he had an amazing grasp on shields. Whatever he might have been going to tell her was shut tightly within his mental shields once again. A hollow space remained where their connection had held.

John stood. He stalked toward the prisoner, his muscular body sliding into motion with a dangerous focus. The Gathan's eyes tracked his movements, but he couldn't follow him as John stepped behind the alien's position, and Sarina noted the darker blue glands on his neck swell in tension.

John was not a lawyer. The truth of the statement couldn't be more evident as she watched him circle the Gathan again. He was a predator, stalking his prey. He leaned in closer to the pirate from behind. "Why did you attack us?" His voice was deceptively casual.

Sarina leaned against the wall and watched. She might learn as much about John as she would about the Gathan—more, perhaps. She already knew the Gathan's motivation.

"Fuck off, *zschtck.*"

John leaned in from the other side. "Why did you target us?"

The Gathan clamped his mouth shut.

"An interesting point in Gathan physiology is their sensitivity to pain," Sarina commented.

John's eyes met hers. For the first time their gray depths reminded her of the Inar icelands.

A microknife seemed to materialize in John's hand. He pressed the back of the small blade against the skin of the

Gathan's neck, probably unaware that he was a mere finger width away from the first of the alien's secretious glands. Even nicking one of those organs could cause more agony than a broken bone.

The Gathan held perfectly still. Dark lines of color ran along his neck and cheeks.

"That is an interesting bit of trivia." He flicked the knife up and sliced a shallow cut along the Gathan's nose.

A shrill noise pierced the air, and the Gathan jerked back until his head hit the edge of the chair. The pirate shuddered as John held the knife perilously close to his face, waiting until a single drop of blue blood dripped from the thin blade.

"They mostly act as spies since they joined the Raveners, not warriors."

"Another interesting bit of trivia. Perhaps our friend here has some other facts he would like to add to our little chat."

When his comment was met with silence, John struck again, a quick slash on the prisoner's check, missing the secretious gland by no more than the width of the blade. The Gathan howled in pain. The *L'inar* along Sarina's shoulders stiffened and flatted wildly in reaction. She'd killed hundreds of opponents, and she'd been forced to question others when the Examiners were not available to do the job. But observing torture was never a welcomed experience.

John didn't seem to react. He had done this before, she knew from the way he handled the blade. What was he—a human from a warrior class the Inarrii were not yet aware of? Or a member of the human militia? The question haunted her. He'd lied to her about who he was. Understandable, if he'd done it out of duty. But the real question was—what *else* had he lied to her about?

"Your skin slices like butter, Gathan. Like butter softened to the point of melting. I could peel your hide from you with this little knife, pull it from you like a glove from my hand." John still sounded casual, so soft, but the chill in his eyes had saturated the air.

Sarina repressed a shiver that threatened to run along her spine. His *m'ittar* remained closed off—she prayed to the gods that he wasn't enjoying himself.

"*Zschtck* pig, you are a primary target," the Ravener nearly shrieked as John held the blade directly against the dark blue center of his cheek gland.

"Why me?" John toyed with the knife where the alien could see it.

"You are in a key spot. But we know who you are."

Sarina didn't change her stance, didn't move a muscle. Who was John Bennings?

Chapter 9

Sarina was watching him. John ground his teeth in frustration. He had no choice. The Gathan was about to break his cover, but he had to discover what they knew and how they knew it. He dragged the back of the knife over both of the prisoner's cheeks. The flesh was different there under the skin and from the alien's reactions he suspected he was threatening a vital part of his captive's body.

"Who am I?"

"Starforce. An undercover agent. And in the perfect place to die. We kill you and the Treaty stops." The words rushed from the alien.

"How do you know this?" John demanded, pressing the back of the knife harder into the blue skin until it creased under the pressure.

"The Terran group has an insider—I don't know who it is. But the spy knew *you*."

John stole a glance at Sarina. She hadn't changed her position, leaning casually against the wall as if none of this was news or none of it was important. But the truth was that it would change everything. Someone knew who he was and had turned the information over to a group of terrorists. Who and why would have to wait, but not for long.

"What do you mean, it would stop the Treaty?" Sarina straightened and took a step toward them. "John's alias is a midlevel negotiator. If he died, nothing would have stopped."

The Gathan didn't reply, so John dug the tip of his knife into the edge of the darker area on his cheek, gouging a mark until the alien began to scream. Then he pulled back and waited. The shrill noises eventually faded into whimpers. A finger of nausea wormed through John's belly, but anger kept him going. This being had probably killed the human he was posing as, at the very least, and was trying to set the entire Earth up to be raped of its resources.

"He and four others will be at the signing of the Earth Accord between the major forces of the human planet. It has to be complete before the Treaty with the Confederacy can be signed. If those negotiators die, the Accord will never be. No Accord, no Treaty."

Something didn't seem right. John stared at Sarina and she looked back at him. She'd taken the truth of his position in stride, never blinking or revealing that she hadn't been aware of his true identity. For the first time he tried to speak to her, mind to mind without being in physical contact. It felt odd, like he'd entered the room naked and with a target painted on his chest. *"He's lying."*

"So were you. But his lies are going to cost lives." Sarina walked over to the main control panel and placed her palm on the glowing ID pad. Immediately he felt the hum of amplification through their *m'ittar* link and shut his side down. She was pissed and about to do something that would probably hurt him as well as their prisoner if he didn't put his barriers back up.

His timing must have been perfect, or maybe she did care at least a little about shielding him from what she was doing, because as soon as he raised his mental shields the

Gathan convulsed in his chair. John pulled away from him as the pirate thrashed against his bonds and howled.

"What is your mission?"

A rank odor seeped into the room, coming from the creature in distress. The Gathan screamed. Even through his shields, John heard Sarina's mental voice pounding against their captive's mind.

"What is your mission?" Sarina demanded again.

The Gathan screamed for another long moment.

"What is your mission?"

Finally, he broke, the Gathan's surrender palpable despite the psychic context. John thanked God and fought back the urge to wipe sweat from his forehead. One more second and he would have pushed Sarina away from the controls. He glanced at her. It was a good thing she was behind the Gathan and the alien couldn't see her. Her usual golden skin had paled and she looked close to being sick. From her appearance, one more second and she would have given up the interrogation.

"We had to find the targets and replace them with Gathan spies…sabotage the Accord, but only long enough for the rest of our fleet to arrive." The alien gasped for breath, his blue skin now riddled with patches of dark blue and gray. "Then, at the final Treaty signing we would break cover and assassinate every one of the human leaders and the Inarrii."

"You were going to pretend to be one of us with this?" John pulled the glowing neckpiece from his pocket.

"Yes. You were the perfect target—take you out and we knew there would be no one to stop the final attack from the inside." The pirate seemed to recover his breath. "Now kill me, *zschtck* filth. Kill me and go on to your human hell. You're too late to stop us."

The pirate began to hiss, the sound evil and poignant to John's ears. An alien show of contempt or mirth—he wanted to smash the Gathan until he couldn't make the noise any longer. Sarina beat him to it, coming over from the control panel from behind the Gathan and knocking him hard in the head with the pommel of her *dash'tet*. The Ravener slumped unconscious against the force-bindings holding him in his chair.

SARINA SWALLOWED CONVULSIVELY AGAIN and again. Her body wished to heave up her last meal in reaction to what she'd just done. She'd been trained to interrogate and, if required, to use her *m'ittar* as a weapon. But she'd never actually *done* it until now. It seemed as though the vileness of the act coated her skin and mind.

"Let's get him somewhere where we don't have to watch him every minute." John didn't look at her as he spoke. Was he as repulsed as she was by her actions, or was he feeling guilty for lying to her, for keeping a mask over who he really was? If that was the case, he didn't need to worry. Inarrii made poor liars and spies but that didn't mean it wasn't ever done, or that she couldn't understand that he was doing his duty. That was a warrior's life. How she felt about it personally was more difficult.

"The storage closet in the corner should have enough room for him." Sarina walked to the corner of the control room and ran her finger over the seal on an almost invisible line. A door slid open. Glancing inside, she noted the closet had been stripped of nearly everything, probably during the partial closure of the tiny base. "This will do."

John hadn't moved; he was staring at the Gathan prisoner. Sarina strode back to the captive and released the force-binding across his chest. She grabbed him as he fell forward and then hauled his unconscious body over to the closet. The force-bindings remained active on his legs and arms, so she checked the cuffs to be certain they remained tight against the pirate's blue skin. The bindings were independently powered, so as long as the cuffs remained on the captive, he would be held in whatever position she posed him. She left him sitting on the closet floor and secured the door to her personal DNA code. He'd be out for a while and by then they would hopefully have been rescued and he could go to the Examiners.

Sarina glanced over at John. For all intents, they were alone again.

"Sarina, I'm sorry—"

"No time for that. We need to warn the other targets," she interrupted, speaking the words aloud. *M'ittar* didn't feel comfortable, not after what she'd been forced to do to their prisoner.

"If we send out any communication, there's a chance it'll be picked up." He hesitated. "I…sent a message out via what should have been a secure channel earlier. It is possible, though, that they knew the codes and found us that way." He paced the room. "If he was telling the truth about there being an inside operative for Terran Purity inside Starforce's Special Agency, then they could be watching for more communications. At very least, they'd know we survived the attack and maybe they'd come looking for us again."

"One of your own has betrayed you."

"Yeah, and I'm beginning to get an idea of who." He slammed a hand against the wall. "It's that fucker, Davis. Has to be." He glared at her. "We have to get out of here. We have to go after the other targets and find out if they've already been switched."

"We can't do it. The medtech shuttle doesn't have a lot of power. It was only meant for short hops and we blew a lot getting here in a hurry. We'd be outgunned by just about any ship out there." Sarina ignored John's anger. What good would fighting do? "We will have to send a message—we can use Inarrii codes this time and contact the base on Jupiter's moon. We can warn them and request an escort. They'd be here in about two hours." She began to check her fighting harness and gear. Two hours was a pretty big window for a second attack. "We'd better grab some supplies and set up a defense for the wait, then send the message."

"Sooner or later someone is going to come looking for that Gathan." John's voice resonated with tension. "They knew we were here so I'm betting on the sooner, rather than the later. We should get the hell out of here and go after the next target. They won't be expecting that."

"If we die, no one will know what the Raveners have planned. We need to pass the info on and prepare for an attack," she countered. "Then we'll go after them."

He stared at her. She could see the conflict in his shoulders, and in the tight line of his jaw. "We."

"Yes, we. You have your assignment, apparently, and I have mine. We do it together or not at all."

"I don't work with a partner. The one guy I thought was on my side has just proven himself to be not only a complete asshole but a traitor to the entire planet."

"Well, suck it up. You have a partner now." Sarina crossed her arms and fingered the arm holsters of her *dash'tet*.

Either the comment or the implied threat seemed to strike him as amusing. Sarina hid her sigh of relief as the atmosphere immediately relaxed between them. "Suck it up? Where'd you learn that? No, don't tell me. Same place as you picked up 'paper-pusher.' I really hated that one, you know."

"The linguistics tables for your language are extensive. How about geek? Nerd?" Sarina teased John as she finished checking her harness for damage from the last attack. She looked up to find John staring at her, his expression serious.

"I had a partner once. He died."

He was telling her something important. A part of her wanted to reach out to him, touch him, but she realized that if she did, he might shut her out once again. "We have all had partners die. Knowing our bunkmates lives are in danger during a mission brings focus to our actions. We risk not only our own lives but those around us."

"He got caught in crossfire. I tried to protect him, but there were snipers in the upper levels of the building we were in." John paced the room.

"You did your duty."

"But he still died. And while I tried to reach him, the target escaped. The mission was a bust."

"That is regrettable, but might still have been the outcome whether you acted differently or not." Now she did step closer. John was more like her than she'd imagined. He carried the weight of a warrior.

"If I concentrate on protecting my partner, I can't do my job."

She reached out and caught his arm, stopping his restless pacing. "You must trust your partner to care for himself as he cares for you. Trust me."

He stared at her, swallowed hard as he thought about it. She waited. She could see the tension in his jaw muscles as he made the decision.

"Okay, partner." He put a hand over hers where she gripped his arm. "What next?"

"There should be rations and water in the upper panel beside the door. I say we go back to the hydroponics lab and set up a barricade. With the oxygen-generating machinery there, combat will be restricted."

"If it worked once, it could work again."

"*TEL SHO AHOI.* This is *Soryen* Sarina Tariim." Sarina spoke into the communications module in the hydroponics lab, using a mixture of human and Inarrii languages she thought John could easily follow. He was her partner and deserved to hear her report.

"*Inar tel sahiir, Soryen* Tariim. What is your status?" The remote patch from the hydroponics log to the control room comm pad held.

Sarina sighed in relief. She was trained in every kind of warrior art, but not in data mechanics. She glanced around the room as she framed her answer. The green glow in the hydroponics lab did nothing to hide the drying blood on the floor. "We are alive. John Bennings and I have taken refuge in the Inarrii moon surveillance base. We were attacked by Terran Purity ships, aided by Gathan technology. We have obtained vital information regarding the attacks."

There was some shuffling as the commtech indicated he was bringing a higher level of officer to the channel. She wasn't surprised when Commander Jannii Finar spoke into the line. "Can you confirm the Gathan involvement?"

"More fully than I would like to. There was one in the party who followed us into the base."

"I see. No hope that you didn't kill the cold-skinned pirate, I suppose."

A wave of relief swept through her at the humor in Finar's tone. He wouldn't be joking if they weren't already mounting a rescue. "Actually, I wrapped him up in force-bindings just for you." She sobered, remembering the way she'd compelled the prisoner to talk. "His body is mostly whole. But you might need an Examiner to put his mind back together."

"We'll do what we have to, just as I suspect you have done. An escort is already on its way. We sent one out after your last transmission, although we weren't sure which sector to search."

Sarina took a deep breath, feeling an ache in her chest, one she'd experienced dozens of times yet still seemed unexpected. "I regret to report that our initial escort is dead. Two *sho'tet* have flown their last."

"Word has already passed to their clan. You may provide your final messages when you are back on board the Osprey. Your new escort is considerably more heavily armed."

A scraping noise sounded from behind her. Sarina glanced back to see John dragging a bench to add to the barricade with one arm. His injured arm hung useless on the other side of his body. Anger flashed though her as she watched him, followed closely by a twinge of shame.

"I must also report that John Bennings is injured. Nonfatal. Please have a medtech available as soon as possible."

"We will have one ready for your arrival."

John joined her at the panel. She nodded to him and then continued her report. "There are apparently three other targets involved in the Terran/Ravener plot. I suggest you quarantine the rest of the human legal personnel. Search them for Gathan technology, specifically holographic equipment."

"Understood." There was a short period of silence. Sarina wished the patch could have allowed for video contact as well as audible. Then Commander Finar spoke again, apparently having checked an incoming data stream. "The medical team requests that you also be ready for inspection and transfer upon reaching the base, Tariim. I am sure the stress you have been enduring has been extreme and you will require immediate attention."

"Actually, Sergeant Tariim has performed perfectly," John interjected. "I don't believe she is stressed in any way."

Sarina glanced at him. He gave her a grin that could only be described as gloating. She shook her head—he didn't understand the seriousness of her injury. The medtechs were only trying to help.

"We can discuss this at another time," Sarina spoke before John could say anything to extend the conversation. "*Tel sahiir denay.*"

"*Tel sahiir denay.*"

Sarina closed the channel. She turned away from John,

took a few steps before she felt him following her. Her stomach churned. Sex, as commonplace as breathing or sharing a meal, suddenly felt like the last thing she wanted to discuss. The medtechs would be all over her when they reached the base. The thought of being examined and possibly tested for response again made her grit her teeth.

She *had* reached completion with John, but she had no real idea why. It could have been any number of things, and now the medtechs wouldn't leave her alone until they knew why. It was their duty, and it was hers too, if she could help other Inarrii to avoid the fate she found herself in—basically cut off from her clan, written off their honor role as finished.

Something tasted bitter in her mouth. What if they couldn't figure it out?

"What's wrong?" John reached to her through a weak and stuttering *m'ittar*. The power of his mind was growing, enough that he could contact her now without touch.

"It doesn't matter. Are we ready?" She tried to distance herself from him. Discussing her discomfort was the last thing she wanted with him.

"We're ready. Nothing to do but wait."

She noted the sardonic tone of his thoughts. *"Your favorite thing to do and mine."*

He got closer to her, looked into her eyes. *"Want to know my favorite thing to do while I wait?"*

Her *L'inar* ridged under the tickling edge of her hair. *"I think I know."*

"I don't know…I'd be surprised if you know how to play poker." He walked away, missing the surprise she knew must show on her face. His *m'ittar* faded as he moved toward his bag of belongings and she found she missed his warmth.

She had to smile when he produced a small packet of what she recognized as playing cards.

"There are rules to this game," he commented aloud as he took a seat at a small workstation at the edge of the room, as far from the door and the traces of the earlier attack as possible. She joined him, bemused at his sudden change of attitude. He seemed almost happy while she was left to ponder his necessary lies and their unlikely future.

"I know a little. There are wagers for each round," she offered as she pulled a bench from a nearby station and took a seat across from him.

"Oh yes, indeed there are."

John's voice held an odd note, and Sarina frowned. "What will we wager with?"

"How about we combine the game with a little truth or dare?"

"I'm not sure I understand, John. What is this all about? What does it have to do with the mission?" She watched him mix the cards between his hands, favoring his injured arm slightly. Eventually he dealt out several cards to each of them and placed the rest in a spot close to mid point between them.

"Nothing. It has nothing to do with the mission, Sarina." His gray eyes met hers.

She sucked in a breath at the intensity she read there. He wanted her, and her *L'inar* rippled in response, but there was something more in his expression than desire. He confused her. Perhaps it was a cultural difference, but she found herself more bewildered by his behavior than before. He broke the connection first, looking down at the cards he now held in his hands.

"Ante up. One truth."

"But I don't know the rules." Sarina picked up the cards, looked at the odd pictures on the faces, the differences between the cards. She recognized the numbers but that was all.

"Doesn't matter. I'll help you."

Sarina licked her lips. The conversation was confusing, and she had no idea what he wanted from her. His offer to help—it could break her if she thought about it too long. What was he proposing? She'd never needed help before and what she needed now was more complicated than he could imagine. The surreal scene, playing cards as they waited to be attacked or saved, it was similar to a hundred missions with Inarrii bunkmates she'd experienced over the years—the forced intimacy brought on by life or death moments mingling with impossible hours of anticipation for the next battle.

"I'LL GO FIRST THEN. One truth for the ante—that's the initial stake. Are you in?" John waited for her response. She needed him. She just didn't want to admit it. He was certain of it now, after seeing her face when her commander told her she would have to face the medical team. He might be in physical pain but it was minor, only a flesh wound, while she had something injured deeper within. She was a soldier; she'd tough it out. But he felt a dull throb in his chest when he thought of her facing them alone. What she'd said earlier, about being thought of as permanently damaged and that she would eventually lose her mind, was shit. She was the toughest, strongest woman he'd ever had the pleasure to meet, let alone touch.

They were good together. Like partners ought to be.

"One truth," she agreed. "What now?"

If he was playing the way he'd like to, he'd be betting for her clothes. His hand was already damn good and seeing her naked again would be delicious. But they only had an hour before they'd have company again, maybe even less if they were attacked. This might be the only chance he had to play for something more than sex. He laid a card face down on the table and drew another. "I'll wager one dare. My hand is good. You can fold—give up now, or you can ask for more cards. You are trying to get as many of the same suit, hearts, diamonds, clubs or spades as you can or a run of them in numerical order. The higher the numbers or faces, the better, except an ace beats all." He showed her his hand. Four jacks. She was finished.

"I'll take two cards."

John raised his eyebrows, keeping his tone light. "Okay. What do you bet?"

"Another truth. I think you owe me a few."

John winced but dealt her the cards. "I'll call. That means I want to see what you have, and the best hand wins. What have you got?"

She frowned and laid her cards on the table. "Only three of the nine cards."

"I win then. You owe me a truth and a dare."

She shifted in her seat and looked away. "Let's play again first."

"No, I don't think so."

She stood and walked away from the table. "This is ridiculous. Playing games when we could be attacked at any time."

It was an excuse and he knew it, could feel it within her. He gathered the cards and put them back in their case, then stowed them away in his shipsuit side pocket. "I've seen the *sho'tet* playing *Haisto*. Soldiers are the same, everywhere. At times like this, distraction is everything." He eyed the curve of her back; her shoulders were tense. "You won't honor your bet?" He was playing dirty but this was important. She hadn't had a chance of winning. He had no intention of losing.

She stalked back to him. Her lips turned down in an angry grimace. He could feel her emotions pushing against his mind. Frustration, sorrow. He slid slowly into the mind contact that had begun to feel more natural to him. *M'ittar.* Beneath her upset he found her fear, and a simple layer of desire. He stepped closer, leaned into her. She didn't move —perhaps she was surprised as he pushed his desire through the link. He held tight to his urge to help her. She didn't need to feel that from him, not yet.

He closed his eyes and touched his lips to hers. Immediately he felt a line of pleasure drawing across his neck and skin. Her pleasure, reflected against his mind. He tasted her, licked the lower edge of her bottom lip and sucked it slightly into his mouth. She opened for him, her lips parting so he could slip his tongue into her mouth to dance against hers. She made a small whimper and he knew she was with him.

"Tell me a truth. Why do you think you'll lose your mind when we already know you can come, you can orgasm with me?" He recalled the experience of their mirrored reactions and slid his memory of their shared orgasm through their *m'ittar*.

She sagged against him, trembling with the power of it. He shuddered too; his cock was so hard he thought he could come right there, sharing this thought with Sarina.

"I'm not sure about why it happened. It might not happen again. Maybe it was the electro gel."

"I don't think so." Thoughts raced in circles through his mind and he fought to keep them separate from Sarina without losing the link. She was wrong, although what that meant for them, he wasn't certain. He tried for a light tone. *"You owe me a dare."*

"Males. Much as I would like to experiment with you, now is not the time for sex."

"Then take me in your thoughts to somewhere else. I read that some Inarrii can do that."

"Some can. It depends on the strength of your gift and the kind of link we would have. I am not sure…"

"Are you going to negate your wager? Keeping her off balance seemed to be working.

Sarina leaned her body into his, nestling into his arms. He held her. Nothing else seemed real. The space around them faded away until he could feel only her touch, the silk of her skin, the soft drag of her hair against his cheek.

"I can't take you to a different place. But I can give you this." Her mental voice had gentled, warmed as she spoke directly into his mind.

He opened his eyes. There was nothing now around them, only emptiness. He looked into her deep green eyes and realized he could feel her naked body pressed against his. No shipsuits, no weapons lay between them. Her ridges ran stiffly erect over the skin of her back and he stroked them so he could watch the desire darken her eyes.

Sarina knelt and lay back, never taking her hands from his skin, never breaking contact with him. He followed her down, although part of his mind shied away from wondering just what they might be laying on. *"Is this real? Any of this?"*

"Shh."

She reached for his cock and he lost the question as she stroked him, explored his member. Under her hands, lines of pure pleasure radiated down the length of his shaft in curling designs. He glanced down for the pleasure of watching her touch him and was shocked to see thin ridges of skin rising along his cock.

"What the hell?" He almost jerked from her touch but she held tight to him, and the ridges radiated pain and pleasure both until he moaned.

"This is only m'ittar dothal. *A dream. Anything can happen here."* She stroked him harder and then rolled, pulling him along with her until she could pin his hips to the ground with her weight. She writhed against him, rubbing her breasts against the thicker skin of his chest. He gripped her arms and pulled her moth to his. She met his kiss and sucked hard at his tongue. Slowly she levered her body until her wet pussy pressed against the tip of his cock and he realized he didn't care what kind of things she would do to him in this dream world; she could decorate his entire body with ridges, as long as she'd ride him, right now.

He thrust upward and met the heat of her pussy. She rocked down on him and they both gasped as they experienced together the intense penetration.

"Sarina, I'm not going to last."

She laughed, the sound painting lines of ecstasy along his chest through the borrowed experience of her *L'inar. "You're not meant to."*

The thought was lost; everything was lost as they

rocked together. He rolled her over and thrust harder into her, pausing for only a second to grasp her breasts and pinch the nipples hard. She wrapped her legs around his waist, pulling her knees upward until she formed a tight sheath around him. He ground into her, lost himself to the tightening in his balls and the feeling of orgasm gathering behind the pressure. She called out his name and he felt within her the same mounting tension.

They mounted the peak together. He pulled out at the last second, her orgasm clenching her tight against him, and pumped hot come over her skin, feeling the heat against his own belly. They sagged against each other, gasping for breath. Their hearts pounded a matching rhythm and for a moment, John thought their very souls breathed as one.

Chapter 10

J ohn opened his eyes. They were kneeling on the floor, both fully clothed. "What just happened?"

"M'ittar dothal. A shared dream. Great for having quickies." Sarina stood and took a few steps away from him. A small part of his mind noted how she shook slightly, leaving him there on the floor.

He hadn't meant for this to lead to sex. Not again. He wanted something more from her, needed it. And he believed she needed it too.

The watchdog unit in his pocket began to buzz. Someone was at the main hatch. It didn't matter what he wanted; evidently he wasn't going to get it.

Sarina opened her mouth, but before she could say anything more to him the patched comm unit beeped, clicking open a channel through the interior intercom system. *"Inar choksan.* This is *Inar Soryen* Yatchim. *Soryen* Tariim, please enter your identification code and clearance."

Sarina walked over to the unit and tapped in a series of codes. Apparently the person on the other end was taking no chances. *"Inar tel sahiir, Soryen* Yatchim. We are in the hydroponics lab." She shut the channel. "It has been a pleasure, John Bennings."

"John Norton." He responded almost automatically.

She lifted her lips in a small smile but he felt it—a sense that what they had together was coming to an end. He wasn't certain if the impression was coming from her or was his own. An edge of panic cut at him. Something wasn't right.

Sarina turned away and began shoving aside some of the things they had used to create a barrier against a second possible attack. He joined her and they worked together in silence. She did the majority of the lifting—his arm had begun to throb again as soon as they'd left the waking dream.

"I will have to report your true position to Commander Finar." Sarina commented as calmly as though she was still playing poker. He wondered for a moment if she still was. "I will wait until I can give my report with a degree of confidentiality. Your cover will be secure."

"As secure as it can be when someone's already handed over my identity to the terrorists or the Raveners. Or both."

"I am certain you will do your duty."

John sat on the bench beside hydroponics tank two—the same place they'd played with the electro gel. He felt unsettled as he watched her pull away the last of the barrier. The one time they'd actually taken things all the way might be their only time. A dream didn't count. He wanted her and she was shutting him out. He had no sense of her mind seeking his. He should be concentrating on the next step in his mission—identifying Davis as a mole and removing any last threat to the legal team. But he watched her and his thoughts felt…empty. Alone.

In another moment the Inarrii team was through the door, and a medtech was helping him onto an antigrav stretcher. Sarina spoke to an Inarrii warrior and he couldn't hear what they were saying. Things were moving and he was no longer a member of the team; he was the charge, not the keeper. He closed his eyes. For the first time he couldn't care less.

THINGS MOVED FASTER than she expected, but in the same direction she'd calculated. Sarina sat in the medtech lab on the Horneu, finally experiencing a moment's peace. She'd been rushed here the moment they arrived, her reassignment from bodyguard to "unassigned" applying the moment she greeted *Soryen* Yatchim at the surveillance base. Nothing less than she'd predicted; the job of guarding John had gone to an Inarrii warrior with a full and untarnished ranking. And she was being poked and prodded as the medical staff evaluated her level of stress and pondered her explanation of full release with John's careful attentions.

Sarina reflected on what she'd been able to gather from the constant chatter of the medtechs. The other human members of the legal team had been tested for Gathan DNA and any trace of alien technology, but the search had come up empty. Either the prisoner had been lying, or they hadn't succeeded in infiltrating the heightened level of security on board the Horneu. John remained undercover after a short period of healing, or at least she thought so— there'd been no gossip about his identity, but she wasn't sure that kind of news would have reached her here in medical seclusion anyway.

Commander Finar had taken her report, listened to her discuss her final mission. He hadn't seemed surprised that she'd been able to function on such a high level, defending John and securing a prisoner, but she knew there would be others who would believe John had been the one providing both the physical strength and the strategy to make their escape. He'd listened to her revelations about John's identity with equal composure, so much so that she wondered if he'd already been aware of John's secret mission. She crossed her arms, fought against the mounting level of impatience within.

The sound of rising voices in the next room caught her attention. The medtech lab normally operated on a fairly silent mode—everyone spoke using *m'ittar* and only the hum of equipment broke the peace. She was nearly crazy with it. If she didn't get out of here soon, the stress from being confined would be enough that she'd have to try therapy again, and that was the last thing she wanted.

The door slid open. Commander Finar stepped into the room, quickly followed by John and *Soryen* Yatchim. Sarina stood, the *L'inar* along the back of her neck fluctuating with excitement.

"*Inar tel sahiir, Soryen* Tariim."

"*Inar tel sahiir*, Commander." She nodded at John and the Inarrii warrior standing in the background. "*Soryen* Yatchim, John Bennings." She used John's cover name, not certain what had been revealed and to whom. She held her shields tightly shut. What were they doing here? Her mouth felt dry. She ran the mission through her head. What more would they want from her? Her behavior had been regulation…except for the questioning of the Gathan prisoner. She'd heard little about the blue-skinned Ravener, despite the fact that he would be prime gossip material. Perhaps she had pushed him too far. If his mind had not recovered…

"Tariim, we need your help." Commander Finar broke into her thoughts. "I understand that you are in a difficult position, faced as you are with a long term of medical testing, but we have been unable to flush out any more of the Gathan spies. Despite the probability of Agent Norton's cover being compromised, we have no choice but to put him back into position at the finalization of the human's planetary Accord."

Relief slid through her. Whatever their plan was, it wasn't about her treatment of the Gathan spy. And the commander had used John's real name, not his alias. He must have told them she knew everything. Sarina glanced at John. His gray eyes were unreadable, his *m'ittar* as tightly shuttered as her own, but he must trust her. He'd included her. "Why do you need me, specifically? I understand that *Soryen* Yatchim has been assigned to guard Agent Norton?"

John stepped forward. He looked good, completely healed. A flutter of desire trembled through the nerve lines along the curve of her belly. She thanked the gods that she'd been tired of being stared at while her *L'inar* were reviewed for every reaction and had insisted on a full ship-suit. "None of the humans would be aware, and probably none of the Gathan operatives either, that you have been taken off duty for medical reasons. We need to prove who within Starforce is handing over information. Having you return as my guard makes it look as though nothing has really changed."

"I see." Her mind raced. She would be part of his cover.

"Even more importantly, my mission tech is the prime suspect. I've been trying to reach him, but he hasn't been responding to my contact codes. But he's a ghost, set to hide and follow data streams. He'll be difficult to find. However, he seems to have developed a...fascination with Inarrii sexual customs. I think your return will draw him out."

The Commander continued. "The Human Accord will be signed tomorrow afternoon, and the Confederacy Treaty only a week from now. We suggest you be placed back on duty immediately. *Soryen* Yatchim will be assigned as general protection for the Inarrii legal team set to witness the signing, but he will actually be there to watch out for you."

The room grew silent. Sarina imagined she could hear their individual breaths. This would be her last chance to prove herself. If she could complete this mission, her clan would surely post her back on active duty. The hope was short-lived. Perhaps they would imagine that she was simply stronger than most, that her mind would still collapse eventually. She needed to prove she was fit for duty, permanently.

"Commander, while I understand the seriousness of this assignment, I wish to speak with Agent Norton privately for a moment." She didn't look at John.

Finar nodded and motioned Yatchim to follow him from the room. When the door slid shut behind them she glanced at John. He stood still, waiting for her to speak. She stood and paced the length of the small room. She knew its dimensions far too intimately already.

"I need your help."

He still waited.

"They want me to help you. *You* want me to help. But if I can't prove that I am truly fit for duty, this will be the last mission I ever have."

"But you told them that you...that we..." John broke off, seemingly at a loss for words.

She lifted her hands in an Inarrii shrug. "Yes, and I've had an Examiner corroborate. But it isn't enough." She lifted her hands to her neck. Asking for this...the words were clawing their way from her throat. She'd never once had to beg for help. "I need you to mate with me. I need to be given back my status so that when you move on, I will have my life back."

Her chest felt tight. She needed this one thing from him, but the commander had been right—there was no such thing as simple sex with a human.

"I've already mated with you." His voice vibrated with a depth that made the *L'inar* on her breasts tingle with anticipation. His eyes were dark; he looked at her like he had the first night on board the Osprey, like he could devour her. She opened her mind widely, hoping for some trace of *m'ittar* between them. She needed his desire, but any trace of pity and she wouldn't be able to try this, no matter how much she needed it.

"I need you to have sex with me in the dining hall,

before witnesses." She rushed on when his mouth dropped open in shock. "It won't be permanent. But Inarrii custom will identify us as mates, at least temporarily. Then they won't be able to say I cannot find completion, or that I am going to slowly go insane. There will be visual proof and many witnesses. I will be reinstated. My clan will take me back."

She watched as he clenched his mouth shut. A muscle trembled with tension along his jawline. "I wouldn't ask this, but we have no time to have an Examiner do a full memory recall before the medical tribunal. It has to be now if you want me to help you complete your duty." Her mind raced. What more could she offer him? "Do this with me, and I will help you find your spy. You might not find him without me. And—" she paused, trying to catch her breath or the words that were tumbling from her lips, she wasn't sure which, "—and, if you require it I will pledge a further service to you."

JOHN FOUGHT against the urge to take Sarina into his arms. Her desperation was evident. He glanced around the medical lab and wondered how bad the last two days had been for her. He'd only had to undergo an hour of treatment to heal his arm. She'd been trapped here the entire time and expected to remain, perhaps indefinitely. Here, surrounded my technical equipment and being poked at indefinitely by medtechs, she would certainly go crazy.

She belonged in the world, working, fighting. She belonged beside him.

"Okay."

"Okay? You mean…" She trailed off. He could almost see the thoughts working through her head. "What service do you require?"

"We'll get to that. For now, let's say that we go through

this and find the spy, stop the assassinations and save the world, okay?"

He reached out to her, hoping for a hug. She stepped away instead. He held back the urge to slam his hand against the wall. Asking for a favor, even if she did offer to practically pay him to sleep with her, had clearly been difficult for her. He relaxed, opened his mental shields as he now thought of the walls surrounding his thoughts and *felt* for her.

"We have to do it tonight. Before we go hunting for your traitor. Perhaps it will even pull him out of hiding."

John caught a glimpse of her thoughts. Heated, flushed skin and the wet friction as he pumped within her. Eyes on them, watching. He pulled away quickly and swallowed hard. Thinking about being watched was not a good idea. He'd never been a show-off. But at least her thoughts were on them, and not on honor and duty. The fact that he wanted that…wanted her to be thinking of him, struck him hard.

Then he focused on what she'd just said. "Tonight?"

"Yes. I will order as much electro gel as I can afford—"

"No." He caught Sarina's hand, forced her to look him in the eyes. "If we are doing this, it's just you and me. No gel. No toys. Just us."

She shivered. "What if it doesn't work?"

"It will. Trust me."

He pulled her close for a kiss. She let him, so he tried to be gentle. But he'd wanted to kiss her from the moment he saw her in this sterile place. Not from pity, but from desire. He'd missed her. He tasted her, breathed in her scent. The soft brush of her mind against his felt good. Her emotions were overflowing—fear, hope, joy, anticipation. He hadn't realized how much a part of their contact was through this embrace of the mind.

The door slid open. Commander Finar stepped through. "I see you have come to an agreement. I suggest that we go to my office to make our plans. Your Commander-In-Chief Johaness will be boarding the Horneu in two of your hours, Agent Norton. We'd better be prepared before then."

JOHN SWALLOWED hard as he looked over the main dining hall of the officer's level of the Horneu. The casual setting looked nothing like the usual military mess halls of the Osprey or other ships within Starforce. Small groups lounged around low tables and couches, some eating, some…engaged in various forms of sexual play. Sarina had warned him they would be watched, but there were a lot more people here than he'd expected. There were even a few humans at a couple of the tables, although they seemed more engrossed with watching and eating than participating.

He noticed a few Inarrii wander over to a table to apparently get a better look at a woman on her knees, pressed between two men. All three were naked, food discarded on the table and their *L'inar* forming tight bands of designs along their skin. The largest male held the female steady as the male in the front took her, then pulled out for the other to thrust in from behind.

"Holy fuck."

Sarina took his hand and linked to his thoughts. *"They are demonstrating that they are a mated triad. By having open sex, they make the other Inarrii understand that outside advances would be unwanted."*

He remembered that from the report on Inarrii sexual conduct, mostly compiled from Captain Susan Branscombe's experiences on board this ship. But reading about it and planning to become a part of this spectacle were far different things. He'd never thought himself a coward, but this might prove things differently.

"Forget them. Let's get something to eat."

Sarina led them toward an empty table about a third

of the way into the room. *At least she isn't putting us dead center.* John's mind raced and he felt a bead of sweat forming along his forehead. He took his eyes off the crowd and concentrated on Sarina's back as she led them among the tables. They both wore *pettans* and he admired the design of her auburn-colored *L'inar* lines on her back and the curve of her hip as she swayed with each step.

Watching her, he recovered some of his balance. She needed this. It might only be temporary, but by agreeing to do this he was agreeing to be her mate. She was already his partner. In his mind that meant he protected her, whether she wanted him to or not. Making love to her here would give her back her life. He stiffened his resolve. It *would* be making love this time. She was the partner that he wanted. She just needed to want it too.

After this was over and she had recovered her rank, and the mission was complete, she wouldn't need him. She'd be back to the kick-ass, proud warrior he knew was under this vulnerable exterior. And he had no idea how they could work their lives together, with their own responsibilities, but damn if he wasn't going to try.

They stopped at the empty table. John dropped down onto the low couch. Sarina joined him, but she sat near the edge and he jerked in surprise as the couch moved under them, lifting to support his back and curving around her calves. A small table rotated around the couch and positioned itself under Sarina's hands.

"Distilled *Rothan* for two, and a plate of crusties."

"What's that?"

"Just snacks. And a liquor. I think I need a drink." She smiled at him, but it didn't look right. She was nervous, far more worried that this wasn't going to work than he was worried about performing in public. The realization was reassuring, somehow.

He shifted toward her and the couch accommodated— changing from a back support to a more cupped design. He almost rolled with it, right into her. She responded with a snort of laughter, but her heated skin felt like silk against his. Without thinking, he reached out to cup her breast.

"This seat is a sterali—it moves with you. It's programmed to try and anticipate your needs." Her mental voice was tinted with amusement.

He smiled at her. *"You could have warned me. But I do like where I ended up."*

"Thank you for doing this—"

John broke the thought off with a kiss. He caught her lips with his, held her still and took her deeper. Across his thoughts he sent a wave of desire to her, telling her without words or even images how much he wanted her, to touch her, to devour her. He wondered if she could also feel how he hoped it might not end with the mission, but even that thought left him as she kissed him back. Only the realization that someone was waiting for their attention pulled him back into reality.

A smiling Inarrii female placed a tray of large orange and green flakes on the small table, along with a bottle of amber liquid and two short glasses. She left without a word, but not without taking a roaming glance at their embrace. Sarina didn't move but he felt her tense beside him, and wondered if she was reacting to *his* anxiety. He reached for the liquor and poured them each a drink. The fluid coated the glasses with a thick, clinging viscosity, and he eyed it with an exaggerated suspicion, enough that Sarina relaxed again in amusement.

"Distilled Rothan liquor. And basal chips. I think you'll like them."

"Sarina, I don't care a bit about them. I'm not hungry for anything but you." John sent the statement with as much calm sincerity as he could express. But he took a gulp of the liquor when she said nothing back. Fire burned down his throat with the single swallow and he felt his eyes tear up. The liquor seemed to hit his belly like a lit match, but instead of burning him further it flamed a path of desire straight to his balls. *Liquid courage.*

Sarina sipped at her drink, obviously acquainted with its strength. He took a finger and dipped it into the liquor. The *Rothan* clung to his skin. He reached over to trace the *L'inar* along Sarina's neckline with the tip of his wet finger. Immediately she focused on him, and her nerve lines reacted to his touch, rising in shallow ridges that followed his caress.

He touched his lips to the path he'd created. He licked her, savoring her lemony skin mixed with the heady bite of the liquor. He opened his mind to hers further, let her see herself as he viewed her. Delicious. She lifted her chin and allowed him to lick at her neck. He nipped at the ridges there, and she sighed a breathy moan. The sound drove desire through him faster than the liquor had.

John lowered his mouth to her breast. Round and firm, the thin ridges there enhanced the curves of each breast and drew him slowly to their center, where he found her nipples hard and yearning against his mouth and hands. He pinched her nipples, pulled them between his fingers until her wispy sighs became graveled moans.

He nudged her—her eyes were closed. *"Sarina, lay back."*

She stretched out and the coach shifted, molding itself to her until she lay exposed to him, her breasts thrust into the air and her neckline exposed. John admired the picture she presented—a woman on the verge of surrender. Only one thing marred his view and he began to work at removing the *pettan* from her hips. Behind him he sensed that he wasn't the only one admiring the view.

Sarina lifted her hips and allowed him to pull off the short cover of her *pettan*. He dropped it to the floor beside him and pushed her knees apart. Her naked pussy invited him closer, the thin lines of her *L'inar* as beautiful as if they'd been brushed on by an artist, but he took a minute to collect another finger full of the Rothan. Sarina gasped as he dripped it on the rising ridges that decorated her inner thighs. He leaned into her and felt the couch give way beneath him, almost dividing so he could settle into the apex of her legs. Sarina lifted her head to meet his glance.

Oral sex between Inarrii meant commitment. But only if she took him into her mouth and swallowed his come would they be permanently mated. Drawing her close to orgasm now with his mouth would ensure no one misunderstood his intent.

"Don't..." Sarina trailed off as he licked at her thighs, sucking every drop of liquor off the hardened ridges of her *L'inar*. Whatever protest she'd thought of was lost. Her *m'ittar* opened to his and he felt the first line of pleasure on his thighs as her experience was mirrored onto his skin.

He groaned, his cock hardening instantly inside his *pettan*. It was now or never. Audience be damned. Sarina was his, and he was going to have her now. He pulled at the ties to his *pettan*, finally freeing himself.

SARINA LOST herself to his touch. The Rothan liquor burned slightly when it touched her nerve lines but John's soft tongue licked away the pain in a slow transfer to ecstasy that made her both want to scream and to beg him never to stop. His mouth against her *L'inar* was the beginning of a mating ceremony. He couldn't know what he was doing, what he was saying to her with these actions, but since their goal was to prove a temporary mating, it was enough that she give in to the moment, give in to him. His mental caress was another source of pleasure. She caught glimpses of herself, displayed on the *sterali* couch like the next course in his meal.

They'd caught the attention of a half-dozen viewers; a human-Inarrii mating was fairly new. The humans in the room stared at them as well, probably shocked by the action of one of their own. John didn't seem to care and she absorbed that strength from him, made herself stronger as hope grew within her.

Her *L'inar* had stiffened to their full height. Each touch, even the careless brush of the back of his hand as he reached for more *Rothan,* brought a jolt of pleasure to her and she trembled as he lowered his lips to the final curving lines that traced to the edge of her *sinaa.* When he laid his tongue against the point where the lines intersected, she cried out, *"Ya'sai lenali.* More!"

John dragged his mouth over her, licking her *sinaa* from one end to the other. She reached out, grabbing the sides of the *sterali* until it began to protrude hard edges she could cling to as John ravished her. This couldn't last, she couldn't come yet, but he didn't stop. He sucked at her *sinaa* and slid two fingers up into her core. She convulsed around him. A minor peak of ecstasy, but he didn't allow her to catch her breath.

A murmur of sound caught her attention. A larger number of Inarrii were watching than she'd expected, even though she knew there would be many aware of her condition. They would be curious to see if there was a way to overcome it. She tried to focus again on John. He was oblivious to the crowd, but he knew she'd lost her pace. He rubbed at the joining spot of her *L'inar* and stretched his body out against hers. His cock lay full and heavy against her thigh.

"Sarina. Stay with me." His thoughts were thick with desire and pleasure washed over her like a wave as she realized that through their mirror link he was still experiencing the minor peak of orgasm she'd reached. The sounds of the dining room faded again as she concentrated on him. She ran her hand over his arms, feeling the silk of his body hair. She took her time, touching him as he touched her, each of their actions duplicated by the other as they reacted to her *L'inar* and to his human senses together.

She found it again. That pressure within her, or within him. It wanted to break free, explode in a burst of pleasure. She lifted one leg and invited him inside her. Their minds were one—he knew what she wanted and he rolled his hips to meet her, his thick cock pressing and rubbing against the tight bands of the nerve lines on her thighs. It was impossible to tell where her pleasure ended and hers began.

She rolled over him in a quick move, and the *sterali* flattened under them. She lifted her hips to center herself over him. In a quick plunge she covered him, his cock parting the folds of her *sinaa* as widely as possible. She cried out and her voice met his. She rocked, and he thrust, the friction between them hotter than the Rathan liquor. They stroked together, finding a rhythm that blended desperation and ecstasy. Her *L'inar* were rippling, burning, battering her with pleasure until the pressure within him give way. Like a flood wave, his orgasm released hers and she shuddered above him.

Chapter 11

John held Sarina to his chest. She shivered against him and he pressed his lips against her hair and kissed her. They were still linked. He'd felt everything—her hope, her desire, the exhilaration as she built toward her orgasm and the joy she'd felt as she reached her final peak and toppled over. They'd done it. And he didn't miss the tiny hint of melancholy that tainted her realization that she'd achieved what she wanted.

Carefully he raised his mental shields, enough that he could keep some of his thoughts and emotions private. Perhaps she was concerned their relationship would be over soon. He grinned to himself. No way was he giving up now.

"Mr. Bennings." The address reached him through his thoughts and he looked up to see his CIC had joined the crowd watching them. It was still a crowd, although some had begun to wander away.

John winced slightly as he wondered what CIC Johanness thought of his all-in approbation of Inarrii sexual customs. "Commander Johanness."

"Please, don't get up." Her dry voice had Sarina's nerve lines flattening against him. He wondered if she realized who was addressing them.

"Thank you. I had thought we would be meeting later."

"Evidently. I will see you in an hour."

John watched the small woman stride away and wondered just how red his cheeks must look. What the hell had she been doing in the dining hall? He glanced around the room at the remaining people. Most had returned to their meals or found something new to occupy them after John and Sarina's demonstration. One person caught his attention. A human man, his shipsuit nearly a size too small for the heavy girth of his stomach, sat alone at a table near the corner of the room. His shoulders were bowed and he drummed his fingers nervously against the *sterali* couch. Annoyance and disgust simmered in John's stomach as he realized the traitor they'd been looking for had been watching them, was still watching as they cuddled on the couch.

"Davis is here. That's him over there. Can you alert someone to have him picked up?"

"Absolutely. And, John, thank you."

He kissed her forehead. *"Don't think you're getting off that easily. That was my commander-in-chief here a minute ago. She's going to fry my ass for sure, and you, you are going to owe me yours."* He sent a quick picture of her lying across his lap while he spanked her, and then watched in satisfaction as the nerve lines rippled across her back.

Idly he stroked the swirling curve of *L'inar* on Sarina's shoulder. She snuggled in against him, apparently in no hurry to move as they waited for an Inarrii guard to collect Davis. They didn't have to wait long, and John's mission tech didn't make any objection as they took him away, despite the fact that he hadn't been responding to John's normal contact codes.

"Okay, time to move. I don't think I can handle lying here naked much longer."

"Really? I thought we might stay and enjoy our chips. Perhaps try a little massage..." Sarina trailed off, leaving him with an

image that made getting up a much more embarrassing procedure.

"You are so going to pay for that."

She laughed, a full-throated sound he hadn't heard much of from her. He had to fight the urge to hug her close. *"Much as I like the sound of that, I'd prefer it to be in a more private setting, and after we've dealt with Davis."*

SARINA STUDIED THE HUMAN MALE. He was not what she'd imagined of a terrorist spy. For that matter, he was not what she would have thought John's mission tech—a man who acted as the intelligence behind John's dangerous missions over the years—would look like. Davis sat on the lone chair in the holding cell, his arms held behind him with the familiar glow of force-bindings. He stared back at her. Something seemed off. He didn't seem afraid that he'd been caught.

John waited on the other side of the cell. He'd wanted to come in, but he was too angry to deal with someone who used to be his friend. Sarina was tempted to probe the man's mind, to glean from him what would make him cross a man like John. John was strong, intelligent and honorable—everything a warrior should be. More, John was handsome, attractive to both humans and Inarrii. She admired him, desired him and wasn't disappointed she would continue to owe him after this mission. Her clan would understand that she needed to discharge the service. Perhaps they could work together for some time to come. Working with John would be exciting.

A small sound brought her attention back to her prisoner. Perhaps Davis had been jealous.

The holding cell force field buzzed behind her, allowing Examiner Salis Fiiten to step through the shimmering wall of power. He nodded to her and she shifted slightly uncomfortably in his presence. The Inarrii had tried hard to counsel her, to bring her to a point where she could find total release, but the best he'd been able to do was to help her to meditate enough to find a relaxation point. With John that wasn't a problem, but she had to wonder if the Examiner had a problem of his own since he couldn't find it within himself to initiate a mirror link. With his training it should have been possible, and she was certain now that the rare link was part of her cure.

"Ricardo Davis, you are charged with treason. How do you plead?"

For the first time, Davis looked shaken. His eyebrows jerked in surprise at the Examiner's statement. Before he could say anything, Fiiten continued, "You must be aware that you will be tested for the truth of your words. I will be examining your memories and emotions to verify your account."

"What is this about?" Davis scowled at them. "I demand human representation."

"That is not necessary. These proceedings are being witnessed." Fiiten took a step closer to Davis, extending his hand to touch the human's shoulder. He would initiate *m'ittar* quickly through touch and force the truth. There was no time for polite behavior. The signing of the Human Accord was only a day away.

The heavy human male was sweating now and he strained to hold himself away from Fiiten's touch. But there was no escape—the force-bindings held him against his chair, and that was bolted to the floor.

The force screen buzzed again. Sarina glanced back at the shimmering wall in surprise as John and his Commander-In-Chief walked through the opaque field.

"You have your human representation." Commander Johaness spoke to Davis, but Sarina's eyes never left her prisoner. If anything, he was sweating more now than before, his anxiety reaching a level that was almost palpable.

Sarina glanced back at John and the Commander.

John's face was unreadable, but within his eyes she caught the hint of repressed anger. She opened her *m'ittar* to him and found that their connection had strengthened. He didn't shut her out now, not completely, and she caught the complex emotions within him—confusion over Davis's betrayal and the wish for them all to be wrong about the man's guilt. The repressed desire to protect a man John had worked with for years.

"Did you pass on information regarding Agent John Norton's mission and whereabouts to the group called Terran Purity?" Examiner Fiiten addressed Davis aloud, apparently for Johaness's sake. He reached out and laid a hand on top of the prisoner's head.

"No!" Davis struggled slightly and then held still as Fiiten made contact. "No, I didn't. I wouldn't! John is my agent, my responsibility."

Sarina felt John tremble through their telepathic link. Johaness shifted, taking a step closer to the interrogation chair. Sarina frowned. The human commander was too interested…too close. Sarina's *L'inar* jumped in alarm. The woman made a move to pull something from the inner pocket of her dress uniform.

Time seemed to slow down. Fiiten turned as Johaness took another step toward him and Davis's bound form. Fiiten was staring at the commander, his expression darkening. John made a grab for his officer, only to be thrown backward by an almost casual backhand blow from the woman.

Sarina leaped, tackling Johaness as she freed a small hand laser from her pocket and took aim. She slammed the slender human to the floor. The laser fell from Johaness's grasp, skittering across the tough perma plas surface. The tiny woman snarled in anger and punched Sarina in the face, stunning her with the power of the blow. Realization dawned as Johaness threw her off. This was not a human female.

Sarina staggered to her feet as Johaness surged toward

Fiiten and the helpless Davis. Reaching Fiiten first, the woman slammed a punch to the Examiner's midsection that had him gasping for breath. Sarina pulled the single knife she wore on board the Horneu and dashed into the fray. Swinging hard, she caught Johaness by surprise, managing to stab her in the shoulder with the *dash'tet*, but the weapon lodged in the bone and Johaness lashed out again, kicking Sarina's knee and forcing her to the ground.

Johaness yanked the knife from her shoulder and made a stab toward Davis. Her strike came inches from the human's throat when a blaze of laser fire slicked through her hand and into the side of her head. She dropped to the floor, dead.

For a second, no one moved. Only the sound of their breaths cut the silence. Then the alarms sounded, warning of active laser fire on board the ship. The smell of burnt flesh closed around Sarina's throat. She glanced over at John, who still knelt on the floor, holding the laser.

JOHN STOOD and walked over to Sarina to give her a hand up. The Examiner, Fiiten, bent over the still body of Commander-In-Chief Johaness and seemed to be checking her dress uniform. Davis stared at him.

"Did you actually believe I would pass on intel to a bunch of terrorists? Jesus, John." His mission tech shook his head. "Just 'cause I commented on you getting some alien tail? Now get me the fuck out of here—you almost got me killed."

Fiiten looked up and gave John a weak smile. "You may release him. He has no part of the terrorists, or the Raveners, even if he is a little crude."

Sarina moved to release the force-bindings behind Davis's back. John shook his head as Davis made no move to hide his admiration of Sarina's body. John ran a hand over his jaw where Johaness had made contact with his bone. The woman hit like a ton of bricks. Then he realized what Fiiten was looking for.

"Is she one of them? Is she a Gathan?"

The form on the ground flickered and shifted. He had his answer. Fiiten held up a small glowing device. "I'm afraid so."

"I knew someone high up was doing some dirty shit." Davis stood, rubbing his hands over the skin on his wrists where the force-bindings had held him secure. "That's why I couldn't answer your contacts, John. I couldn't risk someone listening in. I got my ass over here as soon as I heard the CIC was headed this way—I figured it was someone in her staff. Never thought it would be her."

They all looked at the blue-skinned body on the floor. Half of its face was gone, burned away by the laser. "Well, it wasn't her, was it." John heard the weariness in his voice. "She's probably dead. God knows how long they've had her replaced."

Sarina walked to him and touched his arm. He appreciated the comfort, more than she could ever know. The sound of running feet approached. A rescue team on its way, but too late. They couldn't question the Gathan, couldn't know how far the corruption might go.

Fiiten stood. "Let's meet with Commander Finar and discuss the options. The signing of the Earth's first Human Accord is in the morning."

A FULL TROOP of human Starforce Marines lined the edges of the great conference room on the Jupiter Moon base. The base would soon be handed over to the humans, and this was the first step in showing full compliance to the upcoming Treaty. Today's ceremony marked the first ever full agreement of all the Earth governments since the end of the third world war. Today they signed an accord that would allow one representative to sign the human part of the Confederacy Treaty. Every race invited into the Confederacy had to reach this moment before they could become a part of the alliance.

Sarina watched as another member of the human council passed through the scanners set up at the doorway. Each scanner was set to check DNA and search for Gathan technology. If they'd had these in place for Commander Johaness, they might have a lot more information about what would probably be the last chance for the Raveners to attempt subterfuge, and possibly about any chance of an outright attack at next week's Treaty signing.

But there was no time for regrets. She turned her attention back to the man at her side. Agent John Norton. Her mate, at least for now. *"How long will this go on?"*

"Don't ask me. I don't do the paperwork any longer." John's mental voice was warm with his amusement.

"How about we slip out?"

"Perfect."

Sarina nodded to the Inarrii watch officer. He stepped aside, and she and John made their way past the gathering dignitaries. They didn't need to be there any longer. The threat, at least for today, was gone. Already word had spread regarding her status, that she and John had been the ones to catch the Gathan who could have brought today's event to a grinding halt. She had her place back as a warrior, and as an honor-point-earning clan member. She could walk proudly through the halls.

"I'm hungry. Want to grab a bite?" John's comment accompanied an image of the two of them in the dining hall of the Horneu. The thought had her *L'inar* rippling in response. It was a simple thing, to feel desire and know it was going to be fulfilled, but so important. Contentment filtered through her to him through their shared link.

"Let's go to my room. We can share a meal there."

"Good enough. I'm not really ready to provide another show for anyone but you."

They walked through the corridors, and she fought to

keep her pace steady. Desire raced ahead of her, pulled her toward a place where they could make love again. Finally they reached her quarters. She keyed the DNA scan and stepped inside, pulling him with her. She stopped in the main room. *"I need to know one thing. What happened at the dining room..."* She hesitated then pushed the thought of his mouth on her *sinaa*, his tongue and fingers inside her, driving her with pleasure. *"With Inarrii—"*

"With Inarrii," he interjected, *"making love like that means something. It meant something to me, Sarina."* He stepped closer to her, pulled her close until she was in his arms. He leaned against the wall, pulling her weight fully against him.

She grinned as she felt the hardness of him through the thin material of his dress uniform. His mental touch enforced the understanding of how much he wanted her. Slowly, he lowered his head to hers and she thrilled at the way he took his time to brush his lips against hers. Like they had all the time in the universe.

"I want you to come and work with me as a partner. Help me look for more of the dangers to this planet. Help me protect my people." He took their kiss deeper, parting her lips with his tongue and tasting her. *"I want you, Sarina, all of you. On Earth I would say I am falling for you."*

Sarina's thoughts whirled. He wanted her. His thoughts were clear. He wanted her to be with him, and not just for a term of service. He wanted her as a partner, even if she were to be injured again. And he wanted her as a lover. To build something that might become something more than the casual mating of bunkmates. Joy pulled at her, dancing along with the pleasure she felt from his kiss and the way he'd begun to stroke the nerve lines along the back of her neck.

"I want to be with you too, John. As a partner, in and out of bed. And it doesn't matter that we are far from Earth. I am falling with you." She kissed him back, pouring her emotion through their link. *"Let's go to the cleanser. I believe you had a thought in one once. Something I'd like to try."* Sarina made the

decision and sent an image to John. Her, on her knees in the ultrasonic cleanser. The vibrations pulsing though them, and lips on his cock as she made love to him with her mouth, taking him to the edge of *m'itta lensahn.* Someday she might complete the ritual mating, but for now she would promise to explore a life together. He groaned, the sound reflecting his desire. He grabbed her hand and pulled her toward the cleansing room. Through their contact, she realized he knew exactly what she was offering. It was impossible to guess what would happen with the Treaty, but for now he was everything she wanted. There only one week until the final signing, but already violence was growing and the Raveners, now paired with the highly intelligent and cruel Gathan, would do anything to stop it. But for the moment, someone else would watch over things as she and John built an agreement that had nothing to do with anyone else.

Afterword

A Note from the Author About The Inarrii Language

One of the things I loved most about the Inarrii was their language. I've spent some time creating a phrasebook so I could remember from story to the next, and found myself interested in their spelling, grammar, and syntax (so sue me, I'm an editor when wearing a different hat and name).

Here are a few (in order of appearance not alphabetically) from the first three books, expect this list to grow:

Inure – one race of the Confederacy

Chammis – very soft woolen material – ie ceremonial robes – somewhat heavy

Pettan – short legged covering that wraps from waist to knee

Kahemnit dal – a casual swear like shit

Tel sho ahoi – SOS signal

Tel sho ahoi sho amnetii – sos ship down

Sho Amnetii Gohan yi – ship self destruct.

Sinaa – Inarrii equivalent of a vagina

Saiin - Inarrii equivalent of a penis

Inar tel sahiir – A formal greeting between Inarrii meaning roughly "the world's welcome to you"

Commander Jannii Finar – commander of the Jupiter Moon outbase on Europa

Sterali – a couch that moulds to shape, is meant to eat on and make love on

Yessin – noodle dish

Rothan – a wine like beverage

Saiithan – long cylindrical cookies – light, like almond cookies in taste, made from pressed cheese like substance instead of nuts

Tel sahiir denay – formal goodbye

Pet-horin - winter pajamas

Inar tel sahan yowlenaii – a more loving greeting meaning loosely - welcome to our world together, always.

Ya'lenali – my heart – my love

M'ittar densah – form of mind contact that allows the person in the memory to step out of it to review it

Gathan – blue skinned race of bipeds that was rejected by the Confederacy and has joined with the Raveners. They have darker blue glands that change color in reaction to fear.

M'itta lensahn – ritual mating – roughly marriage in a private ceremony

Slam – a drug that increases stamina, speed, even speed of thought, but makes you itch till you bleed and makes you mean everything you say

Tocuh – a type of touch seal

Ya'sai lenali - asking a lover for more – begging for more – asking for more pleasure

Lin'thal – soul

Archats – slimy stinky alien race that lives in hives, attacks in swarms

Dash'tet – fighting knives, exactly as long as your forearm, each warrior has 4.

Haisto - the live adaption of human poker and chess combined with war strategy

dorii-chiksin—a woven cover of sensors and microscopic tools able to penetrate a patient's skin and access their inner organs and tissue without pain.

Inar choksan – attention, official order

Inar sho sahiir – ship responding

Sho'tet – fighter ship, flying blade

Ken stasht – curse: suck shit

Yimnar – deer like animal that lives in the sand dunes on Inar

Zschtck – Gathan insult: no translation

About the Author

Lilly Cain is a wild woman with a deep throaty laugh, plunging necklines and a great lover of all things sensual – perfume, chocolate, silk! She never has to worry about finding a date or keeping a man in line. She keeps her blond hair long and curly, wears beautiful clothes and loves loud music. Lilly lives her private life in the pages of her books.

All of the above is just so much silliness. When not living up to her pen name, Lilly lives in Atlantic Canada, although she spent eight years in Bermuda, enjoying the heat and the pink sands. She returned to her homeland so she could see the changing of the seasons once again. When not writing she paints, swills coffee and vodka (but not together), and fights her writing pals for chocolate (true story).

Lilly is a single mom who loves reading and writing, dabbling in art and loving and caring for her two daughters. She loves romance in all of its varying heat levels. She loves the chilling moments and the humor in her novels as much as the steaming hot interludes. Her stories are an escape and a release, and she hopes that they can give you that power, too.

To contact Lilly and to find out more about her books, reach out to her website at http://www.lillycain.com

Coming up next? *Undercover Alliance - Book 3 in The Confederacy Treaty Series* Releasing in ebook format September 1st, 2020. Check Lilly's website above for dates and links.

Also by Lilly Cain

If the love story in Lilly Cain's *Undercover Alliance* swept you away, don't miss her other high heat books! And, catch a sample of Between Moons, the first of her shapeshifter series, at the end of this book!

Confederacy Treaty Series:

Alien Revealed

The Naked Truth

Undercover Alliance

Honor Bound Coming soon!

Paranormal Romance by Lilly Cain:

Between Moons

Working on Wicked

Return to Me

Contemporary Romance by Lilly Cain:

High Stakes

No Restraints

Coming Soon - Book 4!

Read a sample of Between Moons!

First in Lilly Cain's *Cursed* Series

Prologue

"We'd like to congratulate Ms. Mathews on her recent closure of the largest deal this firm has seen in ten years. Raise your glasses and toast our sharpest nose for business, our shark in these shallow market waters, Ms. Helen Mathews!"

It was a perfect moment. The entire company had gathered to celebrate her promotion to partner, something she'd worked toward for the last few years with little time for anything else. She had the full attention of the company owner. She looked fantastic, and the room was filled with white linen-draped tables topped with crystal and candles. The food was picture perfect, even if she couldn't bring herself to taste it. Her stomach twisted as she waited for his toast to continue and the announcement to be made.

Henry Winfield, President of Multoma, raised his glass of champagne and smiled at the gathered executives at the head table. In turn, they raised their glasses and smiled, although to most observers it probably looked more like the baring of teeth in a pack of wolves, with none willing to show a moment's weakness.

As Helen rose to accept her accolades, a disturbance at the back of the room drew the focus away from her and toward a small group of people. Two young men dressed in jeans and leather jackets pushed their way through the employees gathered in the hotel convention room, making way for an older woman. They rushed to reach the head table where Helen stood and the Board of Directors of Multoma Development International sat.

As they approached, the two men flanked the oddly dressed older woman. She seemed familiar, but Helen couldn't quite place her. A long, full skirt fell to her ankles, with a ruby scarf providing a brilliant splash of color between the skirt and her white blouse. She was weighted down with rings on every finger. Her hair was gray, but she wore it simply pulled back from her face, the long waves falling past her shoulders. Her black eyes flashed at Helen, and her sneering smile was cold.

"Ms. Mathews." The old woman spoke, her clear voice belying any trace of age and certainly reaching all the corners of the room. "It is good to see that you're being recognized as the shark that you are—a predator that would eat its own young."

A collective gasp rippled through the room. Helen sucked in a breath, and lifted her chin in indignation. Heat rushed to her face and she could imagine the redness creeping toward her neckline when she heard a few tittering laughs somewhere toward the back of the gathering. Annoyance had her gritting her teeth as she struggled to produce her usual professional smile. Already there were motions indicating that security had been called, so Helen remained standing, facing the odd group.

"Many thanks for the compliment." Helen controlled her voice to reflect only sarcasm, her intonation poisonous. "An insult so strong must indicate that I've moved up in the ranks of my critics' black list. However, now is not the time to trade respects. Perhaps you could reach me at the office for an appointment."

"I don't think so. We've had our meetings, and you've still ignored our claim to our rightful land. We don't ask for much. We rarely stay in one place, but still, we must have those few places where we can meet and be ourselves. The Rom will always be travelers, but you have taken away one of our last refuges."

As the old woman spoke, Helen suddenly realized who the person before her was. This was the same well-dressed, professional lawyer she'd been meeting with over a land dispute, a dispute involving the very deal she was being recognized for. Bianca Donceanu's people were the Rom—a branch of American Romanians that retained their wandering Gypsy ways. They'd fought to keep the land—said it was their right to camp there annually as they had for generations—when in truth, the land belonged only to the government.

Sounds of approaching security personnel could be heard, and the woman glared hard at Helen and stroked a long, golden chain hanging about her neck. Her voice became more heavily accented, her phrasing more formal. "I curse you now, Helen Mathews. I curse you in the way of my people. I curse you three times as one who devours, as one who bares her fangs against those who would keep their own, and as the predator you truly are."

With a flick of her wrist the Rom woman reached into some hidden pocket within her skirts and pulled out a small bottle. In a fluid motion she flung it toward Helen. Helen stepped back but the tiny flask smashed against the table in front of her, splashing its contents out and upward, spattering Helen from head to toe.

By now, the old woman was shouting, racing to finish the words she now spoke in a foreign tongue before the guards dragged the uninvited accusers from the room. Helen stood frozen, caught in the spell of the Rom curse. She suppressed the urge to shiver, her blood running cold. She brushed her fingers over the flecks of liquid on her cheek. Everyone near her stared in hushed shock, even Mr. Winfield, a man she'd never seen off-pace.

She looked down at her hand and realized she was covered in blood.

Chapter One

"Well, where the hell is she?" David Sherman's voice carried his annoyance clearly to the receptionist on the other end of the telephone. "I've been trying to reach Ms. Mathews all week. Does she *not* want to close this deal? There are at least two other companies I could go to with this. Understand?"

"I'm sorry, Mr. Sherman. Ms. Mathews will be returning to the office tomorrow. I'm sure she'll contact you right away."

"She'd better. We can't sit on this for much longer."

David hung up the phone and raised a hand to his aching head. What had he been thinking of, convincing himself that this woman was the only one for the job? That she was the only one who could make or break this deal? She'd been vague in her replies to his calls early last week, although she'd confirmed that the deal was one Multoma would be interested in. Then she'd simply disappeared. For God's sake, they hadn't even met yet.

Her secretary couldn't even say where she was. Couldn't or wouldn't. David tensed as the thought occurred to him again that perhaps she had taken the idea he'd brought to the table and offered it to another firm. She was, after all, reputed to be absolutely ruthless. Since her apparent desertion after their last discussion, her absence was all he could think about.

David leaned back into his black leather chair, reclining as he considered the very real possibility of a double-cross. He had put together a tasty package of land just waiting for a big enough developer, and a plan to create a new retail and office center in Philadelphia. Would she steal that idea? He ran frustrated fingers though his hair.

She might. It was time to meet the woman in person. Time to get a better feel for her ethics. It was well known that she was strong, smart, and one of the best negotiators in the trade. She'd won concessions for developments from both the government and the public that no one had thought possible. It was because of her that several unused and derelict sections of land, reclaimed from what used to be one of Detroit's largest dumps, were now being developed successfully into a huge science center and hospital. She'd been recognized by her company and made a senior partner, a feat practically unheard of for so young a woman in this field.

David leaned forward and pressed the intercom button to summon his secretary. He looked around his spacious office. He was no small-time operator; he could take on Helen Mathews. If she thought she could get away with stealing the biggest development he'd ever cultivated, she could think again. His corner office with a view in the largest office building in Philadelphia was proof of that.

Sally, his assistant, entered the room quietly. For a moment David admired her. She was just his type: blond, curvy, and willing. And yet, there just wasn't any pull, any excitement, any challenge. Beyond that, he would simply never get involved with someone he worked with. He had more than enough proof that that path led to certain disaster.

"Can I help you, Mr. Sherman?" She paused in front of his desk, and leaned just a tad too far over, David noted. Although he certainly took a moment to admire the proffered view of her breasts, he was familiar with the pose. Women considered him handsome, but it was the power and money he controlled that seemed to be the deciding factor in their interest. Women loved power. It would be nice if someone wanted him for once, not just the money and prestige that came with his lifestyle.

"I need travel arrangements to New York, Sally." David drew her attention back to work. Once, the kind of challenge she was silently offering would have aroused him, co-worker or not. He had to face it—he wasn't interested, and it wasn't because she worked for him. She was much the same as the last three women he'd had affairs with, he couldn't bring himself to start the cycle again.

She straightened immediately and smoothed her skirt with ill-concealed irritation. He ignored it, but what else could he do but pretend her silent offer had never happened?

"I want the next flight available. Book me first class and make reservations for dinner at Ruby Foo's, in a private dining room. I'll be bringing a business prospect, so be sure we get it, no matter what we have to shell out. I'll stay at my apartment, so you know where to contact me."

David rattled off several more instructions and left a list of reports he wanted generated and sent to him in New York. Within a few moments he was on his way out the door. It only occurred to him then that he hadn't soothed Sally's bruised ego. A quick cell call and an offer of the day off while he was gone was all it took. He could only hope that it would go as well with Helen Mathews.

* * *

Helen collapsed with exhaustion into her office chair. Any brief time away from her desk meant a huge pile of catch-up work, no matter how necessary the absence. Nearly a week off for the third time in as many months had left her with an avalanche of paperwork and her secretary and receptionist both looked at her as if she'd abandoned them. She simply could not explain to them why she'd left or where she'd gone.

Only their longtime loyalty kept them from asking too many questions. The two women had risen with her through the ranks of Multoma Developments and knew they owed her for the opportunities they had been given. Not one word had been said, at least not by them, not even when she knew they noticed a change in her appearance as well as habits.

Helen dug through the pile of papers left on her 'in' tray and sifted out the most important of the reports she'd requested before she left. How much longer could she keep this up? Surely, it wouldn't be long before someone higher up noted her absences. She pulled out the numbers on David Sherman's proposal. She'd only had time to skim it before she'd left last week. It was an excellent plan, one that combined land once considered unusable and therefore cheap, and an innovative architectural concept for engineering office space over what was basically a swamp.

She'd pulled all the information Multoma had on Sherman's past operations and on the man himself, and had taken it away with her. There were times when she'd been able to read during her absence, although deciphering numbers proved impossible. Something about the way she processed information around the time of the full moon was very different. There was a lot to review. He'd been a busy man over the last couple of years, and she discovered his ideas had proved quite interesting and profitable for Multoma before, although her personal team had never worked with him.

As for the man, she'd Googled him and found more than she expected. According to the press, he'd never been married, had worked at the same firm until he became full partner, and was a serious contributor to various charities, including wildlife preservation. And yet, he was a hunter, well proven in his skill against wild game. He owned several apartments and condos across the country.

It was too bad she'd angered him by not contacting him last week. Her receptionist told her how irritated he'd been on the phone when he'd found out she'd left suddenly, but she could hardly have done otherwise. That thought brought her full circle.

She pulled off a pair of dark glasses to rub tired eyes. The shades were a near permanent accessory now. She lay her head down on her desk, ready in that moment to weep. It was becoming too hard. Three times now she'd had to flee her office for an extended length of time. Three times she'd lied about it to coworkers and friends alike. One more time and she would likely be facing serious questions from her superiors about her ability to keep up her workload. Her father would be right, and she would fail. She was so tired.

Behind her eyelids she watched again the events of that horrible night replay like a tired movie. She couldn't escape the memory any more than she could escape the reality of her life since that moment. Once a month she changed, and became someone her father would not recognize. She became an animal.

Helen's intercom chose that moment to buzz sharply, pulling her back to the present. A second after she jerked upright, the door opened.

"I'm sorry, Helen…" Sherry Davis, Helen's receptionist, spoke quickly from the hall. "Mr. Sherman is here and insists on seeing you immediately." The middle-aged woman looked angrily over the top of her glasses at the man who pushed his way past her and through the door.

Helen stood to greet her uninvited guest. Her first impression of David Sherman tempted her to frown, although she held on to her pleasant expression as she'd trained herself to do. He was determined, and obviously irritated by her absence and her receptionist's protective attitude. Broad shouldered and thick through the chest, he towered over Sherry. Slightly too long, light brown hair flipped arrogantly over his brow, and a long nose and smooth, strong jaw finished the frame of his face. Only his hazel eyes stood out as exceptionally beautiful; they brought his features together into a very pleasing form.

Before Helen could quite associate this handsome man with the phone calls she'd received a week ago, he was in her office and having his own good look at her. She flushed slightly as his eyes roved, but she schooled her face into a pleasant mask. She was used to being inspected. It was all part of the business she had spent the last five years conquering.

She dressed the part of corporate executive-slash-warrior. Her tailored fuchsia suit fit her perfectly, and its bright color enhanced her pale skin and long black hair. She knew she looked tired, but as he stared at her longer and longer, she couldn't hold his gaze. What was he looking at? Could he see beyond her façade? Wondering brought an uneasy itch between her shoulder blades, but she refused to give in to the urge to hunch down in her chair.

"Ms. Mathews, I'm David Sherman. I'm glad to finally meet you." He extended his hand. His large, tanned fingers enclosed hers and she felt a tingle of attraction. She smiled at him, but sternly reminded herself of the many, many reasons she could not possibly become involved with anyone just now.

"Welcome, Mr. Sherman. I must apologize for not getting back to you sooner. I've been away on a business trip, as I'm sure my assistant informed you. I did, however, review the preliminary figures of your proposal."

Helen offered a chair with a wave of her hand as she lied though her teeth. She took her own seat, plunging into the details of the proposal. Without giving him an opportunity to comment on her absence, she lifted the page she thought indicated profit estimates, grateful that she'd at least had the time to pull the report from the pile of work on her desk and skim it before he arrived.

David reached for the paper, tugging it gently from her fingers. "Great percentages, don't you think? The lead indicators are well over the norm, and the market polls more than prove the need for these facilities in this location. It's hard to believe no one has acquired the land as yet." He smiled, looking pleased. His smile transformed his face from arrogant businessman to a ruggedly handsome man, and again she felt that zing of attraction.

"Yes, the numbers look interesting," Helen hedged. She had no idea what the percentages actually were, other than good.

"I'm glad to see you aren't letting a great deal slip away from Multoma. I was beginning to wonder if you were planning on passing it over to another firm." He looked at her calmly, apparently ignoring the fact that he was practically accusing her of stealing his pitch and perhaps even going behind the back of her own company. After a tense moment, his eyes shied to the left in a self-conscious movement.

"I see. Multoma does not operate that way, Mr. Sherman. Nor do I," she stated calmly. "My time is better spent as a negotiator than a thief." She kept her face composed, but her stomach clenched. So much for attraction. This was only the first of the problems and accusations she'd likely face by having a forced monthly absence from the company. At least the man before her had the grace to eventually look embarrassed by his suggestion. There were many who wouldn't care that they were being offensive, not when it came to business.

"Well, you can hardly blame me for my suspicions. Not after you seemed to disappear. Let me take you out to dinner tonight to make up for it." His attitude changed perceptibly. He was apparently going to accept her at her word. "We can discuss the proposal then, and you can have today to catch up on all the paperwork that built up while you were away."

He stood, and handed back the paper. "This page, by the way, doesn't have any percentage numbers on it." He smirked, just a bit, and lifted an eyebrow. The scent of his cologne—woodsy and male—reached her and the attraction returned, sharper now. "Perhaps you could read the report before tonight. I'll send you my car." He didn't wait for her answer, pressing the advantage of having caught her unprepared for his visit.

"That would be fine," she said as he walked out the door. "Just fine." She slumped back into her chair and held her head in her hands. "Shit. Cocky asshole. Sexy, cocky asshole."

www.ingramcontent.com/pod-product-compliance
Lightning Source LLC
Chambersburg PA
CBHW071720140626
46557CB00012B/977